SPLATTER ME

A Muse Series Novella

MISSY KAYE

Splatter Me
Copyright © 2024 by Missy Kaye
All rights reserved.

No part of this book may be reproduced or transmitted in any form or by any means, electronic or mechanical, including photocopying, recording, or by any information storage and retrieval system without the written permission of the author, except for the use of brief quotations in a book review.

This book is a work of fiction. Names, characters, places and incidents either are products of the author's imagination or are used fictitiously. Any resemblance to actual persons, living or dead, events, or locales is entirely coincidental.

ALSO BY MISSY KAYE

Shape Me

I want you to draw me like one of your French girls.

— ROSE DEWITT BUKATER

Chapter One
I VOLUNTEER

"Stop that leg bouncing and just read his damn letter already," Mariah breaks the silence without looking up from the fourth draft of her PhD thesis. I jolt and the cabernet in my right hand nearly sloshes out of the glass. My left hand, however, continues its steady scroll on the laptop track pad. I hear Mariah sigh when I don't reach for the thin envelope I'd pushed to the far corner of my desk. Within that envelope lies the result of my fifth round of correspondence with Devo, the disreputable masked artist. Much to my surprise, in my last letter to him, I'd offered to be his Muse. *At least, I think I did.*

The sun had set over the course of the hour as I'd scrolled through *Devo's Darlings*, a popular fan page that gets over 10,000 hits a month. I'm probably 1,000 of them, thanks to my habitual refreshes of the mobile site when I think no one's looking. I've spent hours poring over photographs of Devo's abstract paintings—all of them featuring a woman's silhouette in various... indecent positions. I couldn't wait to see when his next work would drop and to read the inevitable commentary. It's easier to do deeper dives of the blog on my laptop at home, but when I do, as I am now, I often find my eyes flicking to my Zenith Award certificate propped up in the thrifted frame on my desk.

About a year ago, I'd won a $50,000 amateur artist prize under the following qualifications:

1. The applicant must identify as a woman.
2. Applicant must not have participated in any painting exhibition previously.
3. Paintings submitted must explore feminist themes.
4. Artwork should employ styles of realism, including but not limited to figurative realism or objective realism.

Of course, my collection also had to beat out around a hundred other qualified entrants, which it did. My exhibition, "As She Rises," and its corresponding prize are my biggest accomplishments to-date. The experience had given me the confidence to continue to pursue my art, and specifically to continue building on the narrative started in my collection: the uphill battle women face in a patriarchal society.

My two sisters and I had been raised by a mother who'd worked three underpaid jobs following the abrupt departure of our father. The fight for child support never ended, even through our teenage years. I've seen the value society puts on women from a front row seat. Conjuring up that collection had been my own therapeutic response to the struggles of my mother growing up. I had been over the moon to show her my award, especially since I'd chosen a less practical course of study than my sisters. The judges of the Zenith Foundation had validated me and my creative direction. I was going to *make it* with my art.

Thanks to the cost of living in New York City, however, I now have just under $11,000 left from the windfall of my Zenith Prize, and I've found that my creative tap is running at a drip. At least I've still been able to eke out a few paintings, and I know that I believe in the subject I'd brought to life with "As She Rises." So why have I also been seeking out correspondence with yet another man who'd decided to profit off the exploitation of women's bodies?

I realize my leg has begun bouncing again, so I pop up from my desk and take a deep breath, hands on my hips. Mariah stills her typing and eyes me. I stare down the letter, noting the small, rounded grooves my clammy fingertips had made in the paper as I'd transported Devo's response up the stairs of our fifth-floor walk-up. If I tear open the envelope, will I find his answer to my offer?

Earlier

A week ago, on the night I'd contemplated making my Muse offer, I'd paced up and down the well-worn floorboards of my Park Slope apartment with, of course, a trusty glass of wine in hand. I'm a person who likes to stay within the confines of what's possible, but I've also found that possibility expands with a bit of a buzz.

I swirled the ruby red liquid in my glass and let the "legs" run down the sides—it was evocative of splatters on a canvas. *Fitting,* I thought. As our correspondence continued, reminders of Devo and his work began popping up everywhere. I couldn't keep him out of my mind. As I watched the drip nearest the rim slide down my glass to join the rest, my mind spun. I was frozen—every muscle in my body taut, yet thrumming with energy.

I could hear Mariah coming up the stairs and I knew what she would say. As an enthusiastic graduate student in psychology, she'd psychoanalyze me into the ground and come to the same conclusion I'd already come to deep down: *I'm going to invite him to Brooklyn, and I'm going to offer him... me.*

Before Mariah could interrogate me, I made my offer in loopy scrawl, shoved the folded paper in an envelope and licked it closed. I placed it by my purse to mail the next morning. There. Decision made.

"Oh, hey there!" Mariah opened the door right as I'd stepped away from the evidence of my rapidly declining sanity.

"Hi," I let out with a shaky exhale. "How was your day?" I turned away from her before she could gather any suspicions from my expression. I've known Mariah for eight years, ever since we were paired as second-chance roommates our freshman year of undergrad at Sarah Lawrence College. I'd been an incoming Visual and Studio Arts Major, and at two months into the semester, it was the longest I'd ever spent away from home. Mariah's first roommate returned to Sichuan Province, China, after getting too homesick. Meanwhile, my roommate had just transferred after getting a late admission to Syracuse, where she promptly joined a sorority. Greek life didn't align with SL's values.

Mariah and I ended up staying roommates for all four years. In a way, we became each other's homes.

"I've gotta dive into thesis edits for a bit, but would you want to do a pizza and wine night?" Mariah said over her shoulder. She was focused on unwinding her checked scarf to hang by the door.

"I've already got a head start." My lip quirked up as I held the glass up over my shoulder.

"Amazingg," she drawled. "And then you can tell me more about your sexy artist friend."

All thoughts returned to Devo. I'd just started explaining to her the previous night who I kept receiving letters from and why reading them made me smile like a little idiot.

"He's not my '*sexy* friend,' I just like his art! Besides, you know I don't know what he looks like," I said and rolled my eyes. "No one does," I muttered.

"Oh, come on, if he makes the kind of art you say he does, he's gotta be hot," she said.

My stomach fluttered. *So, I have a crush on my pen pal. No big deal.*

"You have to show me some of his paintings tonight," she continued while heading to the bathroom.

"Okayyy." I cringed. I knew that meant I'd be sharing *Devo's Darlings* with her. What would she think of his paintings once she saw how explicit they were? Mariah has always been more comfortable with her sexuality than me. Back in college, before we'd even hit Friday during our first week as roommates, Mariah, completely sober, had brought a boy back to our tiny dorm room. I'd re-watched *Dirty Dancing* for the umpteenth time with the volume in my headphones turned all the way up.

I could never put my finger on why I'd always liked that movie so much. Baby and Johnny Castle were from completely different worlds—the two of them being together in real life would never make sense. The good girl-bad boy matchup is a clichéd fantasy... one I was apparently entertaining.

He's not going to take me up on it, I thought back to Devo. *I'm a nobody...* albeit a nobody who'd been exchanging letters for months with the elusive, masked phenom. He's a creative genius. A steamy Jackson Pollock. The next artist of our generation. Okay, that might be a little dramatic. But he *is* famous *and* mysterious, and I love his paintings.

To some critics and many art world enthusiasts, me included, Devo is the hottest up-and-coming visual artist in North America. His enviable status is due in part to his persona but was catalyzed when a famous young pop star was found to have one of his pieces hanging in her living room.

Vogue had sat down to interview Mischa Michaels on camera leading up to last year's Grammys—she'd been nominated for Best New Artist thanks to a slew of addictive dance floor hits. At the end of the interview, the journalist asked Mischa about the striking painting hanging above her couch. It appeared to be a dark silhouette of a woman with soft curves and her head tilted back. Some sort of beaded necklace dangled from her lips and a hand reached between her thighs. Surrounding the woman's body was a cacophony of splattered paint in bold colors: fiery red, royal blue, a rich sunflower yellow. The only mark that cut through the sensual silhouette was a sharp splatter of emerald green that ran through the hand between her thighs. It was provocative and energetic, the building ecstasy of the moment clear.

"Miss Michaels, can you tell me about the painting on your wall? It's very... provoking. And stunning! Absolutely stunning," the interviewer tacked on.

Mischa gave a Grammy-winning smile. "Thank you! Yes, it's incredible, isn't it? I've never felt so beautiful." She tossed her long auburn locks over her shoulder.

"Oh." The interviewer tilted his head, looking between Mischa and the silhouetted woman. "I didn't realize you were the model. Oh, I can see it!"

Mischa raised her hand up to her lips, which now formed a perfect circle. "Ah—" She'd glanced around with heated cheeks, looking at folks behind the camera. "Let's just say I enjoy being a muse." Her confidence quickly returned, and the audience received an answer within her feigned non-answer.

"The artist's name is Devo," she'd ended the interview with, "and he's a genius." She'd blinded the camera with a dazzling smile and a wink.

Sex sells, and so does intrigue. The Vogue editors had heavily highlighted this section of the interview with close-up shots of the painting, including the scrawled signature in the corner. Mischa was America's of-the-moment sweetheart, and so following the release of the interview, the view count quickly climbed into the millions. The public's fixation on the painting and on Mischa's role as the "muse" propelled Devo to contemporary artworld stardom.

Since the video had been uploaded, "Devo" paintings were showing up all over the place. Some had been authenticated, some had been confirmed as copycats—all featured a colorful explosion, paint splattered across a human-sized canvas featuring a female form—"the Muse"—in various forms of ecstasy. No muse ever appeared in quite the same position, nor seemed to depict the same woman. Devo had confirmed as much in a rare written interview for *New York Magazine*.

"All women are captivating, and their experiences are unique," one of his curt answers had read. "It's important to me that the world sees that."

And this is why I love his work so much; why so many women love his work. I know it's salacious, and I quickly click away if anyone's standing over my shoulder, but Devo's art also centers on female pleasure. It's presented as beautiful and revered... trendy, even. People want it in their homes. I want it in mine.

Maybe one day, I thought.

Pleas from women wanting to be Devo's next "muse" have been posted all over the internet in recent months. Some women pair their pleas with sexy poses in moody lighting, while others give renditions of their best *When Harry Met Sally* orgasm on camera. I'd even seen one video of a slinky woman contort herself into some sort of pretzel shape—a silhouette not yet featured. Perhaps one that shouldn't be...

But I've never seen Devo respond to any of these offers, not that he has any kind of known internet presence anyway. His only confirmed digital footprint is the handful of interviews he'd acquiesced to, typically alongside coverage of a new painting. At the beginning of his rise to fame, when pieces from Devo's "Muse Series" first started being unveiled, his commentary had been mysteriously absent. The last four months, however, had been different.

Devo has been on a continent-wide studio tour. Every week or two, he takes up a "micro-residency" at a little-known studio collective somewhere in the US, although he once spent time at a studio just outside of Toronto, and once in Playa del Carmen.

The public hadn't been made aware of his first micro-residency until a member of the press had been invited to cover the unveiling of a new signature piece at a studio in Oklahoma City. All Devo had shared at the time was that he wants to use his moment in the spotlight to highlight local artists, thus the traveling art studio tour.

This statement only endeared him to his fans more. Some of whom had started very popular blogs fully dedicated to tracking Devo's tour and analyzing corresponding paintings as they're released. Each of Devo's micro-residencies is a surprise to the general public until the unveiling of a new piece, after which, Devo disappears again. He supposedly only notifies the studio he's coming to of his arrival.

Lucky for me, I grew up in OKC and a childhood friend of mine, Larisa, is a sculptor in the very first studio Devo had chosen for a micro-residency. She'd passed me the email he'd used to contact the studio and told me not to share it under the threat of certain death. Of course, Larisa wouldn't hurt a fly. But Devo had clearly commanded some kind of respect and gratitude at that studio for her to advocate so strongly, even in jest, for the secrecy of an email address. I'd waited a few weeks, enough to learn of Devo's informal studio-hopping tour, before I worked up the nerve to send something.

I'd been coming back from a subpar date two months ago when I decided to type something out on my walk home. The air was crisp and my tipsy breath had come out in tiny white puffs as I read it back to myself aloud. I'd wanted to make sure my wine goggles weren't too strong before hitting send on my phone.

Dear Devo,

I love your work. Unique, I know. I'm an artist too. Paint is also my preferred medium, although I don't throw it about the canvas. I work out of the Copper Works Collective in Brooklyn. You should come see us. Maybe I could teach you a technique other than splattering.

With love,
Charlotte G. Faure

I fell asleep that night with thoughts of my piss-poor date, not of the random email I'd sent off to a mysterious celebrity on my walk home. So, imagine my surprise the next morning when I woke up with mussed hair, a fuzzy brain and an email notification:

Dear Miss Faure,
 I'm flattered by your kind words. I do, in fact, know plenty of other techniques... However, I'd surely love to learn what you have to teach. My brush is at your command.
 Besides, I've been meaning to visit Brooklyn. I will let you know if I head to Copper Works. What's your address? I prefer pen to paper.

Your willing student,
Devo

I read the email twice over with bleary eyes and a deepening crease between my brows. *Is this really him?* I looked back over what I'd sent late the night before and cringed. *Oof.* I'd been sassy. I had *sassed* an artist I admire! In our very first interaction, too. *Assuming it really was him*, said a tiny voice in my head.
 Larisa had said that this was the email address he'd used to contact her studio before he'd come to visit... and I consider her trustworthy.
 Who knows who the person on the other end of the

keyboard thought I was, but I wasn't about to let this potential luck of a response slip through my fingers. I replied with my address—a twenty-unit apartment building in Park Slope—and the following note:

In case you're a criminal or an impersonator, I will have you know that you can reach me via "pen to paper" at the above address, but it is <u>heavily guarded</u> and may or may not be where I live. I have a doorman, and a protective dog or two. So... don't do anything crazy.

Whoosh. Sent.

Oh my god.

Subject: Forgot my unit #!
#3D. As in, the third dimension.
And I mean it about the dogs!

I was sober and sending even zanier messages than the night before. Most of what I'd said was neither true nor sensical, but I wanted a letter! And at the same time, I felt vulnerable. Was I an idiot to send my address to a stranger? Maybe. My mom would kill me if she knew.

No immediate response.
An hour or two later. Still no response.
The next day? Nothing.

Whoever was on the other side of those emails, I'd definitely scared them off. I thought over my follow-up send, "As in, the third dimension." *Ugh.* I shook my head and looked up at the ceiling.

It had been a shot in the dark anyway.

Coming back from my studio collective that Monday, I'd found a letter waiting in my mailbox. It was inside in a rectangular white envelope addressed to "Miss Charlotte Faure." I flipped it over to the back and, much to my amusement, noticed a soft violet paint splatter across the flap. To a different recipient, this might have looked like a mistake. I, on the other hand, had a feeling it was a calling card. My heart thundered in my chest, beating with anticipation. I looked both ways in the mail room vestibule as if someone was going to spot me with contraband.

When I finally got up to our apartment on the fifth floor, I ripped open the envelope to find a thick piece of white paper, nicely folded. Once laid out, I scanned the few lines of black angular script, ending on the flourishing signature at the bottom: *DEVO*

It was him. *Right??* Oh my gosh. My hands were building up nervous sweat as I went back to fully read the note.

Miss Faure,

I hope this letter finds you and your 1-2 protective dogs and kindly doorman all well. To try to help prove myself, I'll play a round of two truths and a lie with you:

1. *My eyes are two different colors.*
2. *My first painting in the so-called "Muse Series" was an accident.*
3. *I haven't looked you up.*

Your future student and fellow third dimension dweller,
DEVO

P.S. Send your next letter to:
Mark R.
1224 Taylor St, Columbia, SC
Room 301

(Please don't respond to the email address moving forward.)

P.P.S. I like your dimple.

Of course, that letter sent me spiraling. *What was my internet presence like??* I was googling myself late into the night, trying to find anything and everything associated with me—going all the way back to a picture of myself in my high school newspaper. I was featured holding up a painting of a flower vase I'd entered into a county contest (and lost!). To my dismay, I also found an old blog I'd attempted to start when I'd managed to study abroad in Florence for a semester. Nineteen-year-old me had spent months trying to sketch and paint like the great Renaissance artists to little avail.

I suppose my social media wasn't as guarded as I'd suspected either. All my profile photos were at the ready on Google search! So much for privacy settings...

Which pictures had he seen? Which of my cringey art pieces had he homed in on? Or what was I kidding? There's no way he spent more than a brief glance on anything he'd found. I'm overthinking this. But how could I not?! I am *maybe* talking to one of the art world's most notorious artists! He's taking the time to write to *me!* I mean... assuming this really is Devo. If so, who knows how many women he's speaking to through the postal service?

I wrote out a response explaining that his little game of two truths and a lie proves nothing about his real identity. Although, in my obsessive research, I had uncovered a rumor about the creation of his first Muse Painting that did allude to it being an accident. Before overthinking it, my classic downfall, I sent my letter off to the location indicated in the postscript.

Every letter I've sent so far went to a different address, at his request. He never seemed to stop moving, even within the same city. But he had been making his way up the East Coast lately... leaving newly revealed pieces in his wake—each one a "Muse" painting. Some got more attention than others. The most erotic received the most coverage. I analyzed them all. Each painting reveal correlated with the general location of where I'd been mailing my letters.

His next response came four days later, which means he'd replied to mine and posted it almost immediately.

Miss Faure,

The game will prove something when you meet me. I've been in touch with your studio. Thanks for the recommendation. I'll be looking for a collaborator in Brooklyn. Know anyone available? Brunettes with dimples welcome.

Kind Regards,
Devo

P.S. Send your next letter to:
Sam G.
301 South 12th and Spruce Street
Philadelphia, PA
Room 111

Omg, I remember thinking, *does that mean he's looking for his next muse?* Of course he calls them collaborators—it was the thirsty netizens who had dubbed them muses. Devo hadn't named the series, the audience had.

The Present

Mariah left me in our common space about fifteen minutes ago to meet an early bedtime. She holds 8:00 AM office hours on Mondays as a TA for Psych 101. Her parting words to me were, "Don't stay up too late"—paired with a pointed stare at the envelope in my hand. In other words, *stop overthinking it, Charlotte.*

I fan my face with Devo's unopened letter as I look out the window over my desk. The moon is bright—she's in her waxing phase, and almost full. There's not a star in sight, thanks to the light pollution escaping from the bustling metropolis that is New York City. My skin is heated, but when I put my fingertips to the window, I can feel the chill and the glass fogs.

How would Devo respond to my offer? Would he let me down gently? Would he be cruel? I get up to pace again, taking deep breaths. I pour more wine. What if he accepts? Do I just arch my back against a wall and smile?

I pinch the bridge of my nose and close my eyes, halting my movement. Despite being a part-time artist myself, and therefore keeping the company of many over-the-top and eccentric people, I see myself as more reserved. How had I gotten myself into this position? But here I am, going over my written offer in my head yet again.

Devo: *I'll be looking for a collaborator in Brooklyn. Know anyone available?*

Charlotte: *I volunteer. But what's in it for me?*

It was the shortest note I'd ever sent. I hadn't even been sure it was worth the postage.

I roll my eyes as I remember sending those words. As if "a million girls wouldn't kill for this job," like Stanley Tucci says in one of my favorite movies...

You know what?

That's what I'll do to distract myself from whatever this letter says. I'll watch *The Devil Wears Prada.*

Finally, I set my glass down and slip my fingertip under the envelope's flap. I ease open the paper and withdraw the letter inside. My eyes dart to Devo's even shorter response: *"I'll see you in Brooklyn."*

Oh God. I set the letter down on my chipped coffee table

with trembling fingers. *Does that mean*—I bite my lip—*does that mean he accepts??* I don't know. My mind is going in circles.

I settle onto the couch with the last of my wine and prepare to get lost in someone else's world and choices. Plus, Devo's last letter came from Pennsylvania. I have time to mull over rescinding the offer.

Chapter Two
MCARTHUR'S

Monday is going by in stops and starts, as Mondays often do. I'd gotten sucked into a painting starting early this morning—it features a girl walking out of a swirling mist. I don't know where the initial image came from, but I hadn't been able to stop adding to the canvas. I've been feeling creatively stifled lately, so when I was overcome with the urge to paint this girl, I focused in and blocked out everything else—even thoughts of my steadily paying job.

When I see the time, I nearly throw my paintbrushes across the studio and sprint the five blocks from the Copper Works Collective to catch the G train to Williamsburg. Six months ago, I'd gotten a job as a social media "consultant" for an up-and-coming influencer. Harper has wealthy parents, cash to burn and the body of a model. She'd hired me because she wanted an "artist's" eye and had likely found me from the little notoriety the Zenith Award had bestowed on me last year. You'd think it would be an easy job. Unfortunately... catering to the rich and wannabe famous has its ways of wearing you down.

By the time I finish taking pictures of her from every. possi-ble. angle—walking down the street, the sidewalk, up the subway stairs, down strangers' brownstone steps, even with a forkful of salad in front of her parted pink lips—it's dusk. I take a deep breath and force a smile.

"There are definitely some gems in there!" I tell her. She looks relieved, pats my arm and kisses the side of my head.

"You're the best, Char! 50,000 more followers by the end of November, that's the goal!" She trusts me so much sometimes it frightens me, so I try not to steer her wrong. I tell her I'll narrow down the photos to her best options and she can decide which we post tomorrow. I'm brain-dead by the time I leave, but I also have $300 more in my bank account, so I can't complain.

I could go home now, but the painting I'd started this morning is eating at me. I want to start adding more details to the girl in the mist. Is she confused to be leaving the enveloping cloak around her, or is she purposefully exiting it? I'm of two minds about it. I won't know until I start painting in her features. Sometimes the brush has a mind of its own.

Normally at this time of night, most folks from the Collective have left for the day. Those that remain often end up getting swept into a small crusade by our fellow studio member, Alex, to go out and grab drinks. So, I'm not too surprised when I open the door to Copper Works and see what looks like a gathering crowd.

However, upon further inspection, the group does seem a little more enthusiastic than normal. Eyebrows raised, I meander over. Before I can get too close, a hand shoots out from the dense circle and shouts, "Ok everyone! Let's get moving before I grow old, here! Vámonos! To McArthur's!"

McArthur's is a popular Irish pub a couple blocks down. The crowd starts to move toward the door, and thus toward me. The person who'd shot his hand up and rallied the crowd is indeed Alex, a corny yet charismatic sculptor, and the unofficial leader of Copper Works at the moment. At least our social leader. He sees me standing to the side of the group and walks over to put his arm around me. "You coming, Charlotte?"

I hesitate and don't take a step forward with him. My eyes

shoot over to where my canvas is still set up in my typical corner. "Ah, you can finish mystery girl later!" he says. "We have a special guest tonight!" He points a few folks ahead to a tall male figure with light brown hair above the corduroy collar of a jean jacket. A girl with tumbling blonde hair is practically clinging to him on their way out the building. Daisy. She's a decent painter, but... she would flirt with a wall. She keeps looking up at the guy with the corduroy collar then tossing her head back and laughing. What could be so funny? Is he some kind of comedian?

"Come on!" Alex tugs at my arm again. "Just one pint, eh?"

Alex is from England, where pub culture is key to the daily unwind. Or so he tells everyone.

"Uh, sure," I say. "One beer."

When we get to the bar, we crowd into their famous ten-person booth and Alex orders a round of shots, *on him*. This is my least favorite of Alex's tricks. Taking shots gracefully isn't my forte. I start talking to a girl who'd just started frequenting our Collective last week, Minnie. She's on the edge of the booth and sitting to my right. Whenever I turn back to the table, I can see Daisy and her blonde hair moving in an animated state at the corner of the booth nearest to me. I can't quite see who she's talking to, since there are three people to my left, but I'm assuming it's our guest. Alex is across from us and leaning forward with his elbows on the sticky wooden table. He's trying to get everyone's take on the newest dating app and its promotion of polyamory relationships. It's a very Brooklyn conversation.

The bartender comes over with a black circular tray covered in small glasses, each filled with an amber-colored liquid. Likely, tequila.

"Do you have salt and limes?" Alex is quick to ask. *Yup. Definitely tequila.*

"Not my first rodeo," the bartender responds as she pulls a saltshaker out of her apron and moves a cup of lime slices from her tray onto the table. As the group passes around the necessary tequila shot props, I lean to my left and turn to Miles, the only person in Copper Works that actually works with metal.

"Miles, do you want my shot?" I yell-whisper.

"I don't even want mine"—my shoulders slump—"but to live is to struggle," he says as he shoots his back before everyone else, sans accoutrements. My eyes widen. That was... intense.

"Hey, wait for the cheers, mate!" Alex yells from across the booth.

I lean back farther to reach behind Miles and tap Rob, a good friend of mine who's beside him. "Rob!" No recognition. "ROB." Attempt number two. I tug on his sweater. "Please will you take my shot?" I bat my eyelashes with mock innocence. As long as I've known Rob, he's been exclusively into men, but that doesn't stop me from trying my flirting skills on him every so often.

I've never had success with it.

Rob finally notices my antics in the dark bar and furrows his brow in response. He shrugs a hand behind Miles' back, who's clearly spotted someone across the bar that's captured his interest.

"WHAT?" he yells back. I point to my shot and mimic drinking it, but Miles' movements block my final charade. Rob tries to weave his head forward and back to see me over the distracted person between us.

"Who wants to give the cheers?" Alex shouts to the table, which is getting louder as everyone douses the back of their hand with salt.

"Ya'll are taking too long!" Miles points across to Alex. "Be a man and take it straight!" Alex rolls his eyes and waves him off.

Miles puts his hand on my shoulder. "Mind if I scoot out? I see someone I would like to try a line on." He smiles, eyes set on a curvy brunette in a trendy crop top a few yards away.

I scoot on out to let him play the field and then sit back down just in time to catch Alex's exasperated lead-in to a cheers: "Alright, I'll go then. *Again*—" He taps his shot glass on the table then holds it up in the air. "There are good ships and wood ships and ships that sail the sea—" he starts the speech he often falls back on. I'm still attempting to desperately explain to Rob that I don't want my shot and pushing it toward him on the rough wooden table when Alex's speech is interrupted. Someone pointedly clears their throat from the corner of the booth nearest me. It's loud, and too leisurely for the chaos of the moment. The table's volume falls to a hush to hear what our evening's guest has to say.

"Alex, thank you." The young man holds a palm up towards our de-facto leader. "Thanks to all of you for having me here, not only for this night, but for the entire week." He makes a point to look around at everyone in the outsized booth. His gaze lands on me towards the end. One blue eye. One green. Both piercing, even in the dark room. My breath catches and my heart all but stops. He must have seen the blood drain from my face, because before he pulls his eyes away, I catch a glimmer of a smirk.

Two truths and a lie... my eyes are two different colors... That doesn't prove anything... It'll prove something when you meet me. Variations of the words we've exchanged circle my head as it's filled with buzzing thoughts that almost make me feel as if I *have* taken the shot in front of me.

The visitor continues, "I look forward to getting to know each and every one of you and to seeing your lovely creations. I hope I'm able to repay your hospitality." He holds his glass up to the center of the table, a grin on his face and a gleam in his eye. "Cheers to Brooklyn!" And with that, he knocks back his shot. Everyone scrambles to keep up with him and I look up at Rob pleadingly, even though my heart is still racing. Rob, finally understanding what I want, shakes his head with an expression that I can almost hear: *No girl, that's on you.*

I pinch my glass between thumb and forefinger and pull it towards me. A large and tanned hand with calloused fingertips gently grasps my wrist. I jolt, but the weight of the hand on my arm prevents me from tossing the tequila in the air.

"I heard you don't want your tequila, Charlotte," says the visitor. Daisy tries not to show that she's noticed our mystery guest is talking to someone other than her, a girl no less, but her side eye indicates differently.

I half chuckle, half choke on whatever spit is caught in the back of my throat. I pray the Irish fiddle music playing over the speakers camouflages the sound. "Yeah," I rasp. Rob moves forward to talk to folks across the table, so I sway my body to look at the stranger over Rob's back and finish my answer. "I'd rather not."

The undeniably handsome visitor juts his head back towards the table. "Grab me the salt." He smiles. "If you don't mind?"

"No, no!" I feel flustered and my palms are starting to get clammy. I grab the salt and look for lime wedges, but Alex seems to have taken the one meant for me as a second chaser.

I hand the visitor the saltshaker and he eyes me patiently. *God, he's beautiful.* His jaw is chiseled, and his stubble can be seen in the light occasionally shining in from the street. He has a sharp nose and full lips. I'm staring at them when he clears his throat for the second time that night, "Ehem, your drink, milady?"

A small smile tugs at my lips. "Oh, are we in medieval times then, milord?" I say as I hand over my shot glass, again behind Rob's back.

"We can be wherever, and whenever you want to be, Miss Faure," he says with a roguish expression. My heart starts beating quickly again. He'd addressed me as Miss Faure in almost all our letters. This is the person I was writing to. *This is Devo?* I can't comprehend that he could be both the artist that makes such provocative and addictive artwork, and the handsome, cheerful young man in front of me.

"May I take your hand, my dear?" he asks. Confused, but in the trance of his multi colored gaze, I do as he asks. He grips my slightly clammy palm without a flinch. He sets down the shot glass and picks up the saltshaker, then looks pointedly at the soft flesh between my pointer finger and thumb. He catches my gaze and holds the question in his eye. I nod, thinking I know what he's asking, but still in shock. He moves his head down towards the back of my hand, extended behind Rob, and my eyes widen. Our guest looks up at me with his tongue at the corner of his lips. I push myself to nod again and he slowly licks the area above the base of my thumb. The warm wetness and his intentional eye contact have me squirming in my seat.

It only lasts for a few seconds but I'm taking a deep breath to still myself as he pours salt on the dampened area. I look over at him as heat floods my cheeks and I realize he has to collect the salt in the same fashion. Since our table's post-shot chatty high is dying down, Devo efficiently licks the salt off my hand with a hard, flattened tongue and then throws his head back just enough to take the second shot. His eyes never leave mine. Rob jostles and goes to lean back, so before he can cut our connection, Devo gives my hand a quick squeeze before dropping it with a wink.

I clamp my thighs tight, and stare at the other side of the booth, eyes wide and unfocused. What on God's green earth had I gotten myself into?

The rest of the next hour saw multiple rounds of $5 beers (there's a reason this is Copper Works' go-to Happy Hour spot) as well as many shouted conversations from the group. It also contained a good number of side-long glances from me toward the popular artist I'd been, let's face it, obsessing over for months. I cannot believe Devo is here. Am I sure it's him? Was the mystery artist of all those paintings, depicting women in ecstasy, the same person as the grinning man with the ruffled brown hair, sitting just two feet from me? He can't be much older than me either. I try to act normal and speak with the people in my earshot, but I'd be lying if I said I'm fully engaged.

Every time Daisy puts her hand on Devo's arm and laughs, I notice. Every time his head turns in my direction, I notice. Every time anyone at the table addresses him, I tune in to the best of my abilities. What had I missed before the trip to McArthur's? Had he introduced himself to everyone back at Copper Works? What had he said?

Out of the blue, someone snaps their fingers in my face and breaks my long contemplative stare-off with the center of the table. I release my bottom lip from between my teeth and look up at Miles, who's reaching over Minnie to get my attention.

"Hey there girlie!" he yells over the music. "You're in your own little world again! We're here to be social!" He mock-shimmies his shoulders. The girl he'd left the booth for is nowhere to be found. Apparently, he'd struck out his first go at bat. Lucky for him, there's a benchwarmer ready for her chance on the field: plied with a few shots, Minnie is looking up at Miles as if she'd like to run her hands up his shirt. Miles finally sees what I see and engages with the shy young beauty before him. He sweeps into a partial bow and holds out a hand to her. "May I have this dance, Minnie Mouse?" She swats his chest and giggles in the manner of a girl with a crush. He sweeps her away into the crowd of bar patrons beginning to break it down to the late 2000s hit, "Drop it Like it's Hot."

"Hey, can I scoot out?" Rob yells into my ear from behind me. "I've gotta use the little boys' room." I nod my head in response and begin to move out of the booth without turning around. My hypervigilance on Devo's position makes it so that my entire body stiffens at the realization that we're about to have no one between us.

If it weren't for the few rounds of drinks I'd consumed already, I might have joined Miles and Minnie in the dancing area to avoid Devo. But I'm feeling just a little bit brave and so I slide back into the booth. Once I'm settled in the middle of the faux leather seat, I sweep my eyes up to the left and almost immediately meet Devo's gaze. God, his multicolored eyes are... bewitching. Not a word I use to describe most men. I hold his stare for long enough to mean something, but not long enough to really figure out what it is.

I stare down at my lap and take a deep breath—drawing focus by drumming my fingers on the waxy wooden edge of the table. To my nerves' dismay, I notice that the rest of our party is also choosing this time to transition onto the dance floor. The other side of the booth is ejecting person by person, as if from a pez dispenser.

I look up to assess the exodus and see that Daisy is looking between the last few people scooting out of the booth and Devo's face. He's only looking at me. I have a feeling Daisy's not going to feel great about me after tonight's events.

Finally concluding that Devo's attention is lost to her, Daisy also scoots her way out the other side of the booth. And... we're alone. In the corner of a dark bar. While a distracted crowd dances between the tables and chairs in front of us. Car headlights occasionally flash through the windows, highlighting the sharp planes of Devo's face as he assesses me, leaning back with his arms behind his head.

The few times Devo the artist had been pictured next to a Muse Painting, his face had always been partially obscured. At the start of his fame, he'd always been turned away from the camera, or was pictured pulling the brim of a baseball hat down low over his face. In the last few reveals, he'd stood beside his painting, wide stance, arms crossed, head down, with a jagged black mask covering the lower half of his face. I'd never been able to find a picture of him looking up, and believe me, I'd tried. Devo had always remained unidentifiable.

Now, as I look up at him, I think what a shame it is that a man with such magnetic features feels the need to cover his face. I clear my throat.

"So, um, hi." I awkwardly extend my hand, the very one he'd had his mouth to earlier this evening. "I'm Charlotte." He takes my hand in his warm, rough grip and gives me a genuine grin.

"Hi, I'm Devlin," he projects in a deep voice, making sure I can hear him above the cacophony of noises around us. He leans in closer, still gripping my hand. "And I think it's a little late for a handshake, no?" I can feel the heat creeping up in my cheeks again and hope he can't see it in the dark room as he pulls away and drops my hand. "You've already introduced yourself!" he almost has to yell back. Devlin leans back and crosses his arms, taking in the full view of my profile. His eyes run up from my breasts, the side of my neck and then drink in my full face. It feels like he's memorizing me. I feel exposed.

"What do you mean?" I finally manage to get out. My voice feels a bit strained as I try to ride the line between speaking and yelling. He laughs with his head slightly tilted back. The warmth of both his voice and expression as he unwinds his arms from his chest has me leaning in. I feel drawn to him. I don't know what I expected. If this... *Devlin* person, is who I assume he is, then my idea of him was off base. I guess I would have expected someone colder, more aloof. Someone who wouldn't stay with a bunch of struggling artists in Brooklyn at a low-rent bar in a sticky booth. The person in front of me is clearly a man but has an almost boyish charm. I smile in response to his amusement, but still wait for an answer.

He gestures to me and then imitates writing with a pencil. "Your letters," he says back, "I've enjoyed them." There's a moment of silence between us as I mentally review everything exchanged in those letters, ending on: "I volunteer." My heart really races now. Had I really signed up for something without knowing what it entails?

"How do I know..." I trail off, narrowing my eyes as I let my skepticism try to protect me for a moment. I sit up straighter in the booth and cross my arms. We've swapped postures. He faces me openly, softly grinning and up to no good. My walls are ready to go up. I continue, "How do I know that you are who you say you are?" My eyes narrow, detective mode activated. His eyes sparkle in response and he scoots closer to the ice queen I'm becoming. I keep my arms crossed, but I hesitate as his scent washes over me. He smells like a combination of aftershave, acrylic paint and musk. It's a comfortable smell, and something I want more of. I try not to make the deep inhale through my nose obvious. He can't see I'm *smelling* him for god's sake.

"You mean that I'm Devo?" he asks casually. No attempt to hush his tone. Although it wouldn't have mattered in this establishment anyway, no one is trying to eavesdrop and the music is still blaring. I shrug one shoulder and give a small nod. He scoots closer again, to the point where it starts to feel silly to have my arms crossed. I drop my hands into my lap as I look up at him. He keeps his chin up and smiles down at me, enjoying the challenge and clearly not too concerned with making his case. After a long moment, he juts his chin towards Alex, who's fist pumping on the dance floor.

"Your friend believes me," he says. He meets my eyes again, waiting to see if that would sway me.

"Alex is an idiot," I say back.

"Oof." Devlin mock stabs himself in the heart and laughs. "You're tough!"

I purse my lips in an effort to hold back a smile. *No. I'm in control,* I think, *I control my reactions.*

He continues when I don't immediately respond, "He had nice things to say about you, you know—your idiot friend. Said you're talented."

My eyes widen a bit. "You asked about me?"

"Of course." He drinks in my reaction. "I look into anyone I might collaborate with."

That blush creeps back up my cheeks.

"I still don't know that you are who you say you are." And I mean it. I know I can look naïve, but I pride myself on knowing the truth and seeing things for what they really are. No way I'm going to be conned by a handsome stranger—no matter how charming he is.

"You know, I started thinking about this when I first caught a glimpse of you back at the studio." He cocks his head. "Since Devo is my *alias*, I don't think I have any proof on me that you'd accept."

I look to the side. I don't know what proof I'm expecting either. *Hmm.* Maybe our first emails before we moved to his archaic letter-writing system? "Bring out your phone," I say. He winces and places his hand on the back of his neck. Then he shifts his hips and pulls out a tiny Nokia, a cellphone from a prior generation. I offer it, and him, a blank stare. "Does that thing even *have* email?"

"Ah, no." He chuckles as he shifts again to put the two-bit technology back in the pocket of his jeans. "It's a 'burner,'" he says using air quotes.

"What?"

"I try to stay as disconnected as possible"—he looks up and around, away from my incredulous stare—"but nowadays, some electronic contact is a necessary evil."

I shake my head but remain silent. He gives me a sheepish shrug. Ignoring the modern world is, in my opinion, ridiculous. *What would drive someone to isolate themselves like that?* I'm sure people in his life have put him through the ringer for this choice, so I won't pile on... *for now.*

Instead, I remind myself that I have more important matters to get to the bottom of.

Like figuring out who this man is.

How else might I get a confirmation on his identity? An ID card? *No, he wouldn't have a valid ID for a pseudonym.* I could do a signature match... I grab a crumpled white napkin from across the table and pop my head over the top of the booth. I see a pen discarded beside the check for the next table's wings and fries. I stand up on our booth, hoping the waitstaff won't think I'm endangering myself, and grab the writing utensil. As I go to spin and plop back down, I wobble more than expected on the plush seat. Devlin immediately wraps his hands around my lower thighs. I freeze and look down at him, pen in hand. He smiles up at me impishly. His grip is strong and the heat of his hands drifts upward to the apex between my legs.

"Thank you," I stutter. He shrugs and releases one hand,

which he then offers to me so I can lower myself back down more gracefully. I take his hand in mine. Once I'm safely back on the seat, he lets go of my other thigh. I wish he didn't.

"So, what was that for?" he asks, one brow quirked and eyes sparkling. I take a deep breath and try to recover from the buzzing running up my legs. I slide the napkin and pen in front of him.

"Sign your name," I demand.

His eyes remain narrowed as he tries to understand this test. "My real nam—"

"No," I cut in, "your other name."

He raises his eyebrows, tilts his head in acquiescence and clicks open the pen. First attempt on paper draws no ink. He brings the tip of the pen up to his mouth and then stops. "Hmm"—he meets my gaze—"what's in it for me?" The mischief in his eyes evident as he tosses my line from our correspondence back to me. "That is, if you deem my signature matches with this incredibly handsome and talented artist's?"

"Well, what do you want?" I say, holding back an eye roll and biting the inside of my cheek.

"A kiss," he replies with no hesitation.

My cheeks burn and his smile widens.

"You want to kiss me?" I whisper, causing him to lean in.

"Indeed, I do," he responds. "Is it a deal?" He holds the pen up.

"Deal," I breathe, unsure why I've taken so many risks with what I've said to this stranger. He gives a side smile and winks as he wets the tip of the pen with his tongue.

"That's dirty!" I gasp like a child. Who knows where that pen's been?

He gives me a devilish look. "Dirty you say?" He scrawls with a two-beat flourish, holding my gaze. Without breaking eye contact, he spins the napkin to face me. "I can think of worse. And I'm open to it," he says in a low voice. I scrutinize the signature. It looks... right. I pull out my phone and google: "Devo Muse Painting."

He continues speaking to me as I zoom in on a photo of the artist's signature in the corner of a painting.

"The question is"—he continues hovering above me—"are you?" The signatures are damn near identical. And he'd written on that napkin without looking down. Unless he's a psychopath who's blindly practiced forging this name... this man before me is... "Devo," I gasp aloud.

"At your service." He mock-tips an invisible hat. "Glad to meet you, for the third time." I try not to look like a deer in headlights, but my eyes are as wide as saucers and my mouth is ajar. I try to compose myself. He puts his hands up at chest height, palms facing me. "Don't worry, I won't claim my prize now." My heart pounds. He leans in and tips my chin up with a curled finger. "But I *will* claim it."

The second half of the night consists of more drinks consumed by both of us, a short stint on the dance floor, and shared stories about our favorite artists and works in progress. Turns out Devo paints more than just beautiful women. His other work just isn't famous.

There are some nasty looks from Daisy throughout the night, but Devlin keeps his eyes on me. He dances with me, running his hands up the sides of my body as we sway with the crowd to more early 2000s music. He whispers compliments in my ear. It's intoxicating, literally.

"Your hips are incredible," he says while passing around the other side of me, running his hands down my sides. In any other circumstance, I'd feel shy or smothered, but with Devlin, I feel comfortable and adored. I sway even more to the beat, emphasizing my lower curves. We both laugh.

Daisy is dancing with another tall sandy blonde fellow now, but with occasional glares in our direction. She's not even hiding it. Poor girl. She should have been sending her next crush letters in the mail for weeks like me. And did I have a crush on Devlin? Absolutely. I still have a thimbleful of skepticism, and of course, a hearty amount of self-protection mechanisms that could trigger at a moment's notice. But for now, tipsy and shaking my booty at McArthur's in front of an attractive man with a gorgeous smile and an air of ease... I'm just going to savor the fun of the moment.

After blindly belting the lyrics to too many songs played at my high school dances, I finally take stock of the group and realize I've lost Devlin. I crane my neck and see he's back at our booth, leaning on the table. He's looking down and his face reflects a faint glow, presumably from his stone-age phone.

I tilt my head and watch for a moment. He could be texting anyone, a lover even. I don't know what his personal life is like. I stop dancing and take a deep breath, trying not to let my pessimism bring me down from the fun of the last couple hours. Suddenly, he looks up from his phone and glances toward the door, craning his neck. He starts making his way there, cutting through the crowd with a purpose. Leaving, I presume.

My heart drops. He's bailing without saying goodbye to me. I don't know why I thought he'd tell me before he left. There's nothing between us. *We've just fucking met*, I think. Flirting doesn't mean something is owed; I know that. I just thought in this case, it might mean something more. Alex sees my face fall and comes up to me to put his hand on my shoulder.

"You alright there, mate?" he half-shouts. "Something wrong?"

"Yes, yes I'm fine. All good," I yell back. "I'm just gonna go to the bathroom." I point towards the back of the bar. Alex tips his head in understanding. Now it's my turn to cut through the crowds, but in the opposite direction of the door. I'm third in line. I lean against the black wall and tip my head up to stare at the dusty ceiling pipes. The smile that's been flitting over my face for much of the night is now unreachable. I twist the silver ring on my finger and take a deep breath. *I want to go home.* So dramatic! Maybe he had something important to do, like stop a crime... or maybe there's a woman to run to. He could be taken for all I know. I put a hand up to my face as if that could push my emotions back into place.

"Get it together," I mumble under my breath as it's my turn to enter the bathroom. "We'll just have to see." That's something I've been telling myself a lot lately when it comes to both my art and my life: "Let's just see."

While drying off my hands, I stare into the graffitied mirror and then point to my reflection "He doesn't owe you anything," I say to myself. My reflection nods back and I take one step out the door.

The girls' line has cleared out. And instead, I just see Devlin across from me. In the dark hallway. All alone. He's leaning against the wall, one foot up behind him, his arms crossed over his chest.

"You owe me a kiss, I believe." He quirks a smile. My mouth drops open into a little "o."

"I'm cashing in." He reaches for my hand and pulls me a few feet further down the hallway and around the corner, out of sight of the rest of the bar.

"Where were you?" I force out. "I thought you'd left." Devlin gently nudges me up against the wall, scanning my full body up and down like he's memorizing it, once again. A deep rumble emanates from the back of his throat. He grasps both my hands and brings them up to either side of my head. The movement was so gentle, but now that the backs of my hands are on the wall, I realize he fully intends on using his strength to keep them there. I can feel a heat coiling between my legs. I like that he's choosing to keep me here. I swallow when I realize this about myself and look down and to the side.

"Charlotte," he says, his voice gruff. He brushes his stubble against my cheek briefly and pulls back. I meet his eyes—they're disorienting but both absolutely beautiful. One is a light blue and the other a seafoam green. His gaze is piercing, and he no longer looks boyish to me. This is a man.

"May I?" He looks pointedly down at my lips and then back up to me. I nod, shaking like a leaf. My whole body is filled with a want I barely understand. I want his hands all over me, and in me. I want to roll around in this man's aura and have him worship me in return. His attention is enough for my breasts to swell with need. I clamp my thighs tighter together. So, I nod again in response to his question. Because I do want it. I want him.

His lips come in soft at first, getting a feel for me, getting a taste as his tongue gently parts my lips. Our tongues explore each other slowly, sensually. I release a breathy moan and Devlin becomes a little less gentle. Now he's kissing me more fervently, tugging on my bottom lip and then back to exploring the inside of my mouth. He presses the heat of his entire body up against me. I can feel the hard planes of his chest against my breasts. I want to run my hands up under his shirt, but he still has my wrists pinned to the wall. In fact, he's started pushing them farther up the wall until they're about fully extended. A rough hand cups my cheek and I realize he's locked my two wrists together with one hand.

Suddenly, I'm achingly aware of the swollen front of him. It's pressed against me right where my need is also strongest. My hips involuntarily buck off the wall and try to push into him. He chuckles and pulls back just an inch. "No, no, Charlotte, just a kiss, remember?" I make a guttural sound of disappointment and he chuckles again. "I'll take that to mean you're enjoying yourself."

"I want more," I whisper-whine. That's the state I've devolved into. Arguing with a boy I just met that I'd like his dick to be closer to me, please. Preferably grinding up against me as a first step. With many more steps to follow.

Devlin laughs again. "I can see that." He takes that moment to grip my jaw with his free hand and tilt it up ever so slightly. "I love the way your hair tumbles down your neck," he says, mouth just below my jaw. He kisses the soft area where my jaw meets my throat and I sigh. He trails down the side of my neck with kisses until he's at my collarbone. I want him to release my hands, because I want both of *his hands* to be roving all over me.

The control he's taking is both agony and bliss. I can feel the slickness pooling between my legs. His hand drops from my jaw and slides down the front of my chest to the center, between my breasts. I want him to move that hand either left or right, but instead he's still, looking into my eyes, assessing. I crane my neck forward off the wall to see if he's close enough to steal a kiss, but he doesn't meet me halfway, and his arm still holds my wrists up and back.

The slight sting of that rejection has me blushing again.

"I think you enjoyed that, yes?" He looks at me with a knowing smile. "Now, I'm going to let you go, don't come after me!" he jokes, both hands up to his shoulders, palms facing me.

I slowly lower my arms and cross them over my chest. "I wouldn't," I say with a crinkle between my eyebrows and a dash of impertinence. I'm just one complicated ball of emotions tonight. His eyes glitter as he takes in my shifted demeanor.

I clear my throat. "You didn't answer me earlier." I try to pull myself together.

"What?" he asks. Devlin frowns and scratches his cheek, his expression accentuating the fact that he actually looks a little disheveled now. And damnit does it add to his charm.

"You'd left?" I say, only partially sure. "I thought you'd left." I cast my eyes down and wait to feel embarrassed in admitting I'd noticed his whereabouts.

"Oh"—he laughs—"I went outside a while ago to meet my assistant. I had to give him some instructions." He pops his head into my line of sight. "I didn't leave, Charlotte," he says softly. I blink back. He throws up his hands. "I, well, like you." I meet his gaze as he does his best to make his feelings clear. "The somewhat little I know of you, at least." I take a deep breath through my nose with my lips drawn tight. "I wouldn't have left without saying something to you."

"I don't know you very well either," I mumble and look to the side. *What is wrong with me?? Was I not just aching for him?*

Devlin looms over me as I keep my gaze to the side. He leans down and breathes the following into my ear, "Well maybe we can change that, hmm?" He runs a free hand up the outside of my thigh, then brings it inward. My breath catches. He lets his hand lightly run up the center of me. I let out a stuttered sigh and fight the urge to widen my stance.

Instead, I shift my thighs, trying to get some relief for the swollen bits. He looks down between my legs and raises his eyebrows. I say nothing in response to that. He can't know I'm a puddle of need. I don't trust him yet... but I do like him, and I do want him, so the odds are against me.

Devlin steps back and resumes with a normal speaking voice. Back to business. "I think we should collaborate. You volunteered and I accept. You're beautiful and talented and smart and fun and kind, and a little untrusting, which I can't blame you for. So I'll keep proving myself to you. And you can always change your mind." He cocks his head and makes a sweeping you're-free-to-go gesture with his hand.

"Ok," I say. That was a lot to take in. "I'll think about it."

Devlin's smile reaches ear to ear. "That's all I can ask for!" He flicks a look at the watch on his right hand. "And in that case, I better get to my new spot and start my process, I only have a few days you know." He lands a wink. I roll my eyes in response.

I take a couple steps to round the corner when suddenly Devlin's hand is on my upper arm, and he pulls me back to him. I bump into his chest unexpectedly and he drinks in a short kiss. I'm initially breathless, but then my instincts kick in and I kiss him right back, trying to take more than what I was able to moments ago. My enthusiasm even has Devlin backing up a step. He chuckles against me.

"Ok ok, I'm sorry." His warm breath slides across my cheek. "I couldn't help myself."

I smile at that admission. My brief stint at imitating an ice queen is cracking. "Well, I can't blame you for that," I say up to him cheekily. There's some of my flirtatious spark, I thought I'd lost her for a moment. I once again turn to leave, feeling I've gotten some sort of upper hand. But the hand he has banded on my upper arm pulls me back one more time.

"Charlotte, one more thing." His tone of voice low and his grin devilish this time. His eyes still in intensity. "Don't touch yourself tonight."

My eyes go wide and I gasp. I start to stutter in some sort of protest. "That's not something for you to—, I mean, that's not..."

He lifts his chin and looks down at me. "Trust me"—he winks—"it will be better." I'm speechless. He kisses the top of my head and rounds the corner himself, leaving me there, flabbergasted.

Who does he think he is and what does he know?? To turn me on like that and then tell me what to do? An incredibly successful artist, I guess. ...Whose art focuses on female pleasure... Ugh.

I sigh, and I sigh, and I sigh all night. I don't touch myself, not in the way he implied at least. I do cup my breasts and squeeze them, wishing they were his hands instead of mine.

I dream that Botticelli's *Birth of Venus* painting has come to life, and I ask the goddess what it's like to be trapped in one of the most famous paintings in the world. She just winks and laughs like music on the wind.

Chapter Three
DOWN AND DIRTY

I wake up with pounding temples and bleary vision. I'm meeting Harper at 11:00 AM to help shoot a "collab" with her and one of her influencer friends—an aspiring fashion blogger. I lurch upright and immediately regret my decision as my head reels. The heel of my hand finds my forehead. I grab my phone and see it's 10:17—plenty of time to get myself together and be at the location of the shoot in reasonable order.

Thus, I fall back onto my pillow as my body protests my plan to be responsible. The events of last night come rushing back to me in quick succession. Scenes of a tongue on the back of my hand, a warm grip on my thighs, my wrists... my back up against the wall.

A shiver goes down my spine as I remember the matching signature test and snippets of Devo's parting words. "Don't touch yourself" is the phrase that comes back to me first. It hits me like a truck. I can't believe I followed instructions.

I'm already starting to feel the blood rush to all the wrong... or right places while replaying moments from last night. God, that wall kiss was hot...

I could touch myself now... *why am I listening to a virtual stranger?* I think back through all our letters and part of me starts to make an argument that we're not total strangers. Temptation begins to crack open the door before I force it closed with an ungraceful flip out of bed. I have no time for these wanton thoughts. I have to get going.

As I change my underwear, I notice evidence of my, uh, arousal and I can't help myself. I slide just the tip of my middle finger up my center and my whole body shivers again. I want what Devlin didn't give me last night, and for some reason, I stop at that one touch. I'll try it his way... just this once. I don't even have to tell him I listened to him. I'm experimenting.

I leave the Brooklyn Botanical Gardens with an additional $430 in my digital wallet. Not bad! Harper and her friend had both paid me for pictures this morning. "We're lucky to have your artistic direction, Char!" Harper responded when I'd thanked them both for the generous amount. Over $200 an hour, earned while very hungover, is no small wage! While Harper has clearly been doted on by her parents and presents as a bit spoiled and naïve, she always treats me well. I actually *like* her... even if I don't think we'll ever be close friends.

The two-hour shoot with the leggy blondes among sun-dappled walking paths and exotic flowers had been a helpful distraction. I was able to think about whether we should drape a coat over a shoulder or if Harper's friend looked best holding her purse with one hand or two. Nothing that reminded me of the steamy make-out last night or a man's hand grazing the apex of my thighs. I wasn't reminded of stubble against my check or his piercing gaze, or even our upcoming "collaboration."

Well, the thoughts are back.

I make my way over to Copper Works in a haze. I try my best to focus on the scenes I pass: a man feeding pigeons from a park bench, a woman pushing a tiny dog in a stroller, two kids perfecting a secret handshake. However, as I near my destination, I can no longer distract myself from the butterflies beginning to crowd my stomach.

Will he be there? I assume so. If this is where he's hosting his next micro-residency, he must be working on his next project. A project that I seem to have volunteered to help with. "What's in it for me?" I'd asked him in that last letter. He'd never actually answered. If I'm helping him paint in some way... I'd hope to get credit. But I'd never seen a Devo collaborator revealed officially and I'm not sure how his process works.

A jolt of energy shoots through me, helping the Advil and Gatorade I'd downed earlier cut through my hangover. I can't tell if I'm nervous or excited. Probably both.

I cross the threshold of Copper Works and scan the surroundings. There are a few folks milling about or focusing on their artwork. I don't spot the brown-haired, light-eyed boy who'd partially ravaged me last night. My heart drops and the adrenaline dissipates. I take a deep breath and let my muscle memory carry me through my normal routine of preparing to work at my canvas in the corner.

Alex sees me and waves from beside whatever abstract sculpture he's making in his usual spot across the large room. I muster a smile and wave back. Once I don my smock and grab my supplies from my locker, I head to my unfinished painting of the girl in the mist. My eye catches on a white envelope resting on the corner of my easel, leaning on the dry paint. A small paint splatter crosses the front of the envelope. It almost looks like I missed my canvas; it almost looks like a mistake. Once again, I know it's not. The butterflies are back, and they are flapping their wings, *hard*.

I pick up the envelope and look around the room again, to see if anyone's noticed the blush creeping up my neck and cheeks or if Devo is watching me open this from some dark corner of the room. But no—no Devo in sight. No one's eyes are on me. We're all in our own little worlds. I slip my finger under the flap of the envelope and pull it open. The note within contains the same handwriting I'd seen in Devo's correspondence for months—but this letter is quite brief.

My name is at the top in bold, angular cursive followed by a dash. Below is a note simply saying:

> *If you still accept, meet me here tomorrow, noon.*
> —D
>
> P.S. *I'd hold off for another night.*

My eyebrows knit together. Is he implying that I still don't *touch* myself for another 24 hours? Who does he think he is?? And he didn't sign off with his full name this time. Why would he do that? Do I still want to sign up for our "collaboration," as he calls it? An uncomfortable feeling claws its way up my chest, and I run a hand through my hair. I have the urge to stomp my foot like an insolent child, but refrain. Instead, I delicately slip the note back in its envelope and put it in my back pocket. I don't have to decide anything now, even though I can tell my body is already anticipating seeing him again. My mind wants to focus on *my* work, right here in front of me. The girl in the mist. What journey is she on?

Without much to work with from Devo's note, I focus on my art and get lost in the next few hours of added detail and story. By the time the natural light starts to fade from the windows, I think I've realized the girl is on a journey of self-discovery. I go home that night feeling satisfied about the progress I made on my piece, and pretending that I'm undecided about whether I'll show up tomorrow.

Our radiators hiss as I pull a sweater down over my head and warm socks on my feet. The temperature outside just dropped to the legal minimum before our building is required to provide heat. I brush my teeth with one hand and mindlessly scroll social media with the other.

A video comes up on my screen and my thumb stops. I let

my toothbrush dangle from my lips as I use both hands to turn the volume up on my phone and zoom in on part of the video. It's featuring a Muse Painting. But the focus of the video isn't on just the art. A majority of the screen is taken up with a shot of a young woman with long, gleaming braids. She has chocolate brown eyes that are framed by sharp, winged eyeliner, heavily glossed lips and high cheekbones. She's more than beautiful, I realize, she's striking. My brows furrow as I drag the video back a few seconds and lean in with my toothbrush still hanging from my mouth.

"It was quite the experience," the striking woman says as she runs her delicate fingers over the thick braid running down her collarbone and chest. Her posturing comes across as almost... feline. She's graceful, unattainable, intimidating.

Just then, Mariah pops her head in the bathroom doorway. "Hey whatcha got goin on my little *artiste?*" Once I'm in full view, she tilts her head and squints. Her eyes sweep over my unkempt hair I'd hastily pushed back with a terry cloth headband, and the toothpaste dripping down my chin. "Busy week? I didn't see you yesterday."

I pause the video, finish brushing my back molars and spit. I wipe my chin and spin back to face her. She's now looking down at her own phone. "Yes, actually," I say. "I did a photoshoot with Harper today and I worked a lot on a new painting!"

"A new painting!" she says without looking up from her phone. "That's amazing! I know you've felt stuck for a while."

"Yeah!" I turn back to the mirror and take off my mascara with a reusable cotton pad and make-up remover. "I'm kind of excited about it." And that was the truth. I hadn't felt inspired for far too long. Now I feel inspiration coming at me from multiple angles.

"Well, I'm proud of you!" Mariah beams up at me finally, phone down. I have a good four inches on her, although I always felt her stature commanded more respect.

I give her a genuine smile back. I feel so grateful to have a friend who always roots for me. Mariah is a blessing.

"Hey, what did mystery man's note say?" She shimmies her shoulders and purses her lips. "You know, from Sunday night?"

"Ah, he said that he might come to Brooklyn one day," I reply. Which isn't technically a lie...

"Ooo!" she exclaims. "How exciting! We could use a little intrigue in our life!"

"We?"

"Well, obviously I'll need to live vicariously through you once you meet your hot and sexy pen pal." Now her whole body shimmies and she spins on her heel. "How fun would that be?" I can hear her say as she walks away toward her bedroom.

"Good night!" I yell after her. She waves over her shoulder. Mariah can just pop in and out like that, even in large social situations. But she always leaves an impression.

Alright, back to the video. I need something to distract myself from the rising guilt over the fact that I didn't tell Mariah everything going on with Devo. I put my phone down and hit play while I continue to do my skin care. The video cuts to an older gentleman with a gray streak through his coifed hair.

"*Will you finally be the one to tell us how these paintings are made?*" the man asks in a voice made for radio, it was deep and smooth. The woman shrugs with a coy playfulness and sparkling eyes.

"*What I can tell you, David—*" She purses her lips and looks up and around for a moment, swaying her shoulders right and left. "*Is that it was well worth the NDA I had to sign, if you know what I mean.*" The video cuts back to David.

"*I don't believe I* do *know what you mean!*" he counters. "*An NDA is involved, huh?*" A moment's musing passes. "*Are you supposed to reveal the involvement of an NDA?*" He rubs the stubble on his chin. "*I thought, you know, that's something you're not supposed to mention.*"

Back to the woman—she shrugs and smiles. "*All he told me was that I can't reveal his methods. Besides*"—she turns to look directly into the camera—"*I don't know that it would be appropriate for all of your audience to hear about the process anyway.*" She smirks with bravado.

"*We'll be right back after a message from our sponsor—*" The video cuts out. It was a clip from a filmed internet talk show.

I spend the next hour in a digital rabbit hole looking up any additional Devo lore I can find. I go over every painting he stood next to and every interview he'd ever given (a total of two). I stare at the jagged black mask that runs across the lower half of his face in his more recent pictures. The images definitely give a more ominous impression than the one I received from the friendly and bold young man from McArthur's.

I dive into the online forums discussing the likelihood that certain surfaced paintings could be his. Some of the paintings even I can tell are copycats... others, I'm not so sure. Not many "muses" have come forward, it turns out.

At about 1:00 AM, my eyes start to close. I try to keep reading with just one eye open to give my other one a rest, but soon that effort also concludes.

In the morning, I only remember snippets of the dreams I had, including one where I once again speak to a woman in a painting. Except this time, I talk to myself—or the version of myself I'd painted coming out of the mist. She told me to show up tomorrow.

I also dreamed of the hallway at McArthur's, and a man in a black mask with light eyes pressing me gently against the wall. I was wearing lingerie I didn't even own. The man put a finger to my lips as he pierced me with eyes the color of arctic ice. The hallway melted into a meadow and the wall behind me was suddenly a tree. He put two fingers inside of me and I writhed—

My "last ditch" alarm goes off and I wake up in a literal sweat. *Wait*, I think as wakefulness mixes with remnants of the dream I was just torn out of. I quickly close my eyes again. *I think I wanted to finish that dream.*

My heartbeat ratchets up to a rate where I know I won't fall back asleep. The dream is gone, and I know I'm going to the studio today. At exactly the time Devlin asked me to. I have hours to get there. I roll my eyes up to stare at my white ceiling and brush damp tendrils of my hair off my forehead. I shift my hips under the covers and allow my other hand to snake down between my legs. *Wow.* It's rare I wake up *turned on.* Is this what men experience when they have a wet dream?

As I go to pull my hand back up from under the elastic of my pajama pants, my middle fingers skim along my swollen clit and my muscles twitch involuntarily. I gasp and lift my finger so that it's hovering just over the sensitive bundle of nerves. My body's so turned on. I clearly didn't finish getting off in my dream... my brain is drenched with a lust that takes me by surprise. I press my finger back down and draw slow tight circles around my clit. My eyes roll back and my eyelids flutter. I stop thinking about being a responsible adult and allow the chemicals in my body to decide what I'm doing.

I move my other hand down my body, squeezing my breasts as I go, sliding down the side of my hip. I think back to Devlin running his hands down my waist and hips on the dance floor. It had felt so good to be appreciated for my curves, to be so wanted by someone that... I clearly wanted back.

I push two of my fingers into myself and arch my back at the idea that they're Devlin's fingers, like in my dream. I see the icy, silent version of him: Devo with the mask. And then I think back to the lively, warm version of him laughing with his head thrown back in the booth: Devlin—the one whose rosy lips had pressed themselves to mine, whose boyish charm is intoxicating. The combination of these two versions of him turns me on *more.* Who is he? Do both versions of him want me? I hope so. I want both of him.

I'm running my fingers up and down my clit more fervently now, and pumping my other fingers in and out. I can feel my climax building and I don't want to lose it. I allow myself to imagine whatever I want. It's the icy version—Devo—his face fills my imaginary field of vision, and he pulls down his mask to reveal a wicked smile. He curls his fingers into my G-Spot and I allow my fingers to do the same. His hand is around my throat and he whispers in my ear, "I can't wait to see you like this later today."

My muscles spasm uncontrollably and the vision fades. I do finally pull my hands out of my waistband and I lie in my bed, flushed. A thin sheen of fresh sweat covers me from head to toe. Physically, I feel wonderful. Mentally, I'm confused by the intensity of my fantasy, how turned on it had made me.

I'm tugged out of my reverie by the memory of the postscript on the note Devlin left me yesterday: "I'd hold off for another night." Well, I held off for the night, didn't I? It's *morning* after all, and I'd received no suggestions about that. So why do I still feel a touch a guilt? I shake it off and check my phone. I now have an hour and forty minutes to get to Copper Works, and if it was up for debate about whether I needed a shower before, then the answer is clear now.

I ride my endorphin high for a bit longer in the hot shower, but as I go through the rest of my routine, a different tingling feeling extends from the center of my chest. I wish this man had given me a goddamn phone number! But maybe it's for the best he hadn't. That way I can't text him that I've suddenly come down with the flu and can we reschedule for a time when I've miraculously gathered more nerve.

Instead, I take a deep breath and give myself one more once over in the mirror. I don't want anyone else in the studio to give me a second glance, but I want to look at least a little nice. I have on a smokey gray T-shirt, a bit more fitted than my usual choices, and my favorite jeans that I think hug my ass nicely and are marked with paint swipes along the thighs. I finish off with a kerchief around my neck, a common addition for me, and a swipe of red-tinted lip balm, an *uncommon* addition for me. Most days, I'm a classic chapstick girl.

I look like I'm ready to paint, but I also look feminine, and dare I say, tantalizing? At least my curves, often covered by looser clothing and a smock, are on pretty full display. My hair is combed into a purposeful "messy" bun with tendrils framing my rosy cheeks and lightly rouged lips. I attempt my own devilish smile and think about the breathless state I was in less than an hour ago. Now that I'm not quite as pent up as I'd been since I'd left McArthur's two nights ago, I can react to whatever this afternoon may hold with a level head.

Devlin used the word "collaborate." That sounds professional. Upright. Doable. I can always change my mind, he'd reminded me. I leave my apartment in good spirits, buoyed by my confidence in my appearance and my internal pep talks.

This is going to be a breeze.

I arrive at Copper Works at 11:59. I'd never been so punctual in my life. I cast my eyes around the large concrete room, expecting my fellow artists to be in motion and focusing on their separate stations. At least some of them. Any of them? Not a soul is in the studio. Did I get the time right? Are we closed for a day? I was able to get inside though... if we were closed, I'd think Alex would have locked the door to the outside. "Hello—" tumbles out in my shaky voice as I take a few steps inside.

No answer.

My fingers twitch and I have an urge to re-do my hair while I have this moment alone.

Just as I manage to pull out my elastic, letting my coiled hair unfurl, a hefty metal click resounds behind me. I whirl. It's him —he's at the door in his mask and wearing a baseball hat pulled down low. He must have come in after me. Electricity zings through my every limb. "De-Devlin?"

A slightly muffled chuckle comes from under his mask. "Yes, Charlotte it's me. Sorry to startle you."

"No, no, I'm fine." I'm shaking my head back and forth. I cast my eyes to his boots, trying to convince myself that I'm fine as well.

He pulls down his mask and smiles with a hint of an apology, looking pointedly at my hand that I didn't realize had thrown itself over my beating heart. I draw my hand down purposely, slowly. *I am in control,* I remind myself. But as I look up at his face as he drags his eyes up my body, the carnal energy he's exuding has me wondering if in fact, I am *not* in control.

"No one's here," I offer up more meekly than intended. "Normally people are here on weekdays."

"I asked that we have the studio to ourselves today," he says simply. He tilts his head and takes a step toward me.

"Why were you wearing your mask when you came in?"

He smiles and rolls his eyes. "A few bloggers are starting to get wind of my new spot"—he gestures to the space—"I'd prefer they not snap a picture of my face."

"And why is that, *Devo*?" I emphasize his pseudonym.

"Well, *Miss Faure*—" He takes another step forward and I think he's maybe about to touch me, but instead he bypasses me and heads for our small kitchen. He has that same smell of aftershave and acrylic I'd first caught on him at McArthur's.

He yells back over his shoulder, "I'd like to keep some semblance of a private life during this 'fifteen minutes of fame' I've been granted." I can hear him flick on the sink, and when I catch up to the kitchen doorway, I see he's washing his hands.

Devlin runs the soap over his fingers and then thoroughly scrubs it off. He turns to me as he pulls a paper towel and I realize I'm staring.

At his hands.

I look back up to his face and he raises his eyebrows. "A woman of many words today, I see."

He brushes past me once again, leaving me flustered. I'm determined to pull myself together.

Devlin makes his way deeper into our rather large studio. It used to be a warehouse for storing copper and had been equipped for pre-installation welding operations, thus the name, Copper Works.

I hang back for a moment and chew on what he'd said when I'd asked about his mask. "Wait—" I finally jog after him as he makes it to the end of the long room. "What do you mean your 'fifteen minutes of fame'?" The exertion from my jog builds upon my already elevated heartrate, and I land beside him unexpectedly out of breath.

Devlin's not paying attention to my question. Instead, he's opened a door to a storage closet and is visually surveying the contents. Now that I'm just inches from him, I don't know what to do. The last time I saw him in real life he had me up against a wall. And the last time I saw him in my mind, he'd had me against a tree, and had taken things quite a bit further... just thinking about it has me blushing again. Of course, he takes this moment to turn his head out of the storage space and look at me. I adjust my stance and turn my head, trying to nonchalantly obscure my face with a curtain of hair. To my great relief, he keeps any commentary on my shifting energy to himself.

"Apologies," he says, "I normally know what the set-up is going to look like ahead of time, but I had my assistant set everything up for me this morning." I'm confused until he opens the door wider and allows me to see inside. Our usually messy storage room filled with partially used or ripped canvases and forgotten supplies, now looks more like a lounge. An ornate red velvet settee sits in the front of the room; its wooden legs and edges are intricately carved and painted gold. The large circular base that's normally used to roll out large sculptures now has a cream-colored tarp draped over it, with what must be a four foot by six foot unframed canvas laying atop it.

Not only is there a *velvet* couch in our storage closet, there's also a Persian rug covering the cold concrete floor, stretching from the settee to the platform. I spot an ice bucket with a bottle of champagne sitting inside it, and is that... is that *music?* Coming from *where?* I look around, trying to find a source.

My eyes must look wide as saucers because Devlin's rich laughter shakes me out of my stupor. "So, all of this"—he waves at the room with one hand while his other holds the back of his neck—"is actually supposed to make you more comfortable." He squints his eyes at me slightly and tilts his head. "It's not supposed to make you more on-edge." Devlin offers me a sheepish smile.

Once again it feels like he's heavily observing me, memorizing all my expressions and interpreting them all, well, correctly. I *am* a little on edge. And it's frightening that he can just see through me so easily. "Stop perceiving me!" I blush as I force out the first joke that comes to mind. For the first time, it's Devlin's turn to look confused.

"Stop...?" he says with his head cocked.

"Yes, stop perceiving me, I don't want to be *perceived*," I emphasize, chuckling again and concurrently wishing I could just say normal things.

Devlin cuts my self-consciousness short though. In a quick but gentle movement, he pulls his jagged mask back up over his mouth and nose and steps toward me, causing me to bump up against the the doorframe to the converted storage room. He places one hand on my collarbone and one hand on the doorframe above us. The proximity forces me to tilt my head up to look into his light-colored eyes. They're not quite as icy as they were in my dream, but I can see a definite hunger in the way his irises dance across my face, landing on my lips.

"Yes?" I whisper up to him, shaky—my senses heightened. This is a familiar position between the two of us, and I'd wanted more then just as I want more now.

"Hmm—" he muses, and moves in closer to my neck before

running his mouth down to my collarbone. I can feel his hot breath press through the mask and whisper down my bosom. "I certainly hope—" he continues, while shivers wrack my whole body. He moves back up in front of my face and holds a hand gently to my cheek— "that you'll allow me to do more than just perceive you."

He steps away and sweeps into the room. I pry myself off the doorframe and pray that at no point in time this man sees my underwear. He affects me more than anyone I can remember. Past boyfriends be damned. I gingerly step into the storage room and look back out into the larger space one more time to see if there's anyone loitering about. This mysterious assistant, perhaps? Not a trace.

I close the door behind us.

"So, why are we working in here? If uh, no one is out there?"

Devlin's back is turned, and he pours champagne into two fluted glasses he's inexplicably procured.

"I thought it was cozier in here, more amenable to the type of environment I like to work in," he replies over his shoulder.

"But then, why would you need the space cleared? Out there?" I gesture to the door.

"Precautionary measures," he says turning around, handing me a flute of champagne—the effervescence is fresh and dampening my fingers. "Just in case there are sounds we want to keep private." His lips quirk and his eyes alight upon my face for a reaction. My heart leaps but I try not to emote. Instead, I take a sip of my champagne and sit down, crossing my legs and pursing my lips.

"Are you now going to explain to me what exactly you've asked me here to do, Mr. Devo?" I try to take the bold, playful route; I don't want to fall prey to my nerves. I came here of my own accord, and I'd like to remind myself to act with conviction when it comes to my own choices.

"Ah, *'Mister'*." He takes a step in front of me but remains standing, forcing me to tilt my head back to look up at him. He places his pointer finger under my chin, and I see that his mask is no longer on. Now it's his turn to take a swig of the sweet golden drink. "Not my first preference, but I can work with Mister." He winks, and steps away, taking another large sip.

Once again, he's left me confused. "What do you mean? What do you prefer?"

"That's likely for another time." Devlin comes back to sit beside me on the couch and brings up a slate of papers with a pen atop them. "First though, I must ask you to do something. I'm sorry."

I look at the papers and take in snippets of legalese.

"So, an NDA is involved?" I raise my brows and search his eyes for validation.

"Unfortunately, I had an incident earlier on and it was strongly recommended to me that I have each, uh, collaborator I work with look this over and sign."

I take a deep breath. Legal documents aren't my strong suit, and I'd never been one to read the fine print.

"I don't really—" I struggle to respond.

He waves his hand at me. "Don't worry, you don't have to sign it." He looks at me with sincerity. "We just won't collaborate on any art in that case, and that would be fine by me, Charlotte."

I slowly nod as I weigh what he's saying. He continues, "But even if you do sign it, we can still stop at any time." He rubs the back of his neck. "And to be honest, I don't think I'd act upon anything anyway"—he gestures to the paper—"but I'm told it's a deterrent for talking to the press and I, well—" He looks around the room. "I value the privacy of my process."

I think back through all the videos of the young women who'd claimed they'd been a "muse" for one of Devo's paintings. Their eyes shone with the excitement of a secret kept, of a special nostalgia for something they'd never forget. They hadn't seemed traumatized or frightened... or even upset that they weren't Devo's only muse.

Should I *be upset by that?* I wonder. But no—I know I'm not the first. Logically, I don't see an issue. Emotionally... there's something that makes me uncomfortable, and I don't want to explore it. *There is no* real *relationship here*, I think. I set my bristling feelings aside.

As much as I've acted like I'm too skittish to do this, I am here. I am all the way here, in this tiny, decked out room with THE Devo. Because I reached out to him, and continued to write to him, and asked him to come to Brooklyn, to *my* studio, and then I'd found him charming, and mysterious and I'd wanted to touch his body with mine... I am here because of me. And I will continue to be here because it's what I want.

"Let me take a look." I put my hands out for the papers. His face lights up as he hands them over. It's not that I don't trust him... it's just that I've never had to sign an NDA in order to proceed with an art project before... nor with anything for that matter! I'm just an amateur painter, a non-celebrity. A good ole' fashioned, runaway transplant in an artsy pocket of a big city. I suppose I've gotten to this place in life by taking some risks, so what's another one? I believe him when he says I can walk away at any time no matter what. I sign the document with a flourish and down the bottom half of my drink. Excitement rushes up my torso much like the bubbles that had rushed up my champagne flute.

Devo turns back to me after inspecting the unframed canvas lying flat upon the raised platform, almost like a stage. I can also see he's pulled out a few fresh tubes of paint alongside cups and brushes and what I think is a thinning agent of some kind. "You've signed it then!" He throws me a wide grin, his eyes on my signature. "This calls for a proper cheers!"

I extend my flute with a soft smile. I still feel in the dark, but I'm happy to celebrate with him. We clink and Devo sits beside me, he then pivots my body and drapes my legs over his. This feels a bit intimate, but it also feels... good, just touching him. We both smile over our sips of champagne. "So now you're mine for the day." The carnal look is back, and he makes no effort to hide his roving gaze.

"I'm 'yours'?" I counter. Is that what I'd signed off on in the NDA? I hadn't read it fully, but I didn't see anything possessive.

"Yes, only if you want to be, of course." Devo leans in close and searches my eyes. "And in a way, I'm yours as well." He makes a show of casting his gaze away from me. "Only if you want me." Without shifting his head back to me, he gives me a side eye and a smirk. He has a very good guess that I *do* want him. And once again, he'd be right.

I take a deep breath. "Yes, I um, want you." I scrunch my eyebrows, tasting those words as they come out of my mouth. That doesn't feel natural to me—to admit what I want. I look up into his eyes. I can't believe I'm saying this in this straightforward of a fashion. It feels forbidden, to be so honest, but it's lighting up something inside of me that I didn't realize I'd smothered.

"Good!" He swings my legs off him and abruptly stands, setting his glass down. He reaches for mine with a "May I?" expression. I hand it to him, and he sets that one down by the bucket as well. When he rejoins me on the couch, he has a glint in his eye. He clasps his hands and asks, "What turns you on, Miss Faure?"

I blink back my surprise. Nothing about today seems conventional, so I suppose I need to roll with the punches. *His art depicts female pleasure,* I remind myself. This is the inspiration he wants from me. I really think about my answer. "Well"—I look around—"an attractive man helps." I keep my gaze directed away from him, and he laughs. It's a beautiful, husky laugh, and it takes the edge off his mysterious persona.

"I'm flattered," he says with a hand over his chest.

I roll my eyes as he moves forward to kiss my cheek. "What else?" he whispers. He skims the side of his pointer finger down my jaw and I shiver. "You like being pushed up against things I noticed," he says, running a warm hand up my thigh, squeezing lightly just inches from the bend at my waist. My back involuntarily arches with his hand so close to the spot that's already hot and slick for him, uncomfortably so.

"Yes," I breathe, "I do like that."

Devo then swiftly slides my body down the length of the couch by my ankles so that I'm fully laying on the settee. A soft vocalization escapes my lips and I look up at him with wide eyes. I guess there's more to his process than just talk. He laughs again.

Devo uses a knee to widen the space between my thighs on the couch and then kneels down over me, just inches from my face. I can see his arm muscles flex as he grips the back of the couch, holding himself up.

For a moment, I'm disoriented. The way the light falls across his face has his icy blue eye looking at me from shadow, while his green eye appraises me from a brighter angle. Looking between them is like experiencing the switch between Devlin, the young man who's quick to laugh and full of boyish charm, and Devo, the aloof, enigmatic man who hides behind a dark mask and is brimming with desire.

I go to sit up on my elbows and he gently, but forcefully, pushes my shoulder back down and maintains the exertion of force upon it.

"What else, Charlotte?" His eyes are already heavy with lust as he drops light kisses across my cheeks and lips. He nips at my jawbone by the side of my chin. I gasp, not expecting teeth. He pulls up above me and smiles. "What else?"

My heightened arousal and quick intake of breaths have my mind foggy. Devo runs his hand down the side of my T-shirt, tracing my waist in a way that once again feels amazing; the look on his face as he does so is ravenous. Seeing him want me this much is a sexy feedback loop I can barely stand. He slides his hand down further and cups my pussy over my jeans, then presses in. My hips buck slightly and Devo smiles. I slowly lower them back down at the indignity. I both love him enjoying me and hate how closely I know he's observing my reactions.

"Listen," he says in a gruff voice, "I don't want to do anything you don't want to do." I attempt to pay attention through my lustful brain fog, blinking more rapidly to try to get a grasp on what he's saying. God, it's hard to retain information when this captivating man is on top of me. Devo continues, "Don't get me wrong—" He comes in close to my face again and just lightly puts his lips to mine. "There's plenty I'd like to do to you." He can feel me smile against him and he smiles in response. He gives my lips a quick kiss and pulls back to see my face yet again. "But for this to work Charlotte, I *need* to know what you want. And of course, that includes if you want to stop."

I close my eyes to gather my words, aware of my full body flush. "You *need* to know?" I ask. I'd never had someone tell me they needed to know what I wanted. I'm sure people had been *curious* to know what I'd wanted, but no one had ever said they *needed* to know.

"Yes, Miss Faure." He grins. I'd never noticed how sharp his canines are—they make his smile wolfish. "I need to know." He nips my neck and I yelp. I feel we're at a precipice. What way will this scenario tip based on what I say? "We're creating something here today," he murmurs against my neck, running the tips of his fingers down the center of me, between my breasts like at McArthur's, but still not touching them. "And knowing what turns you on is part of the process."

My heart races wildly because I know the flavor of what I want to say, but I'm still afraid to let it pass my lips... and I don't know how to say it.

"What is it?" He looks between my eyes, assessing. I almost wonder if he can see what I want to say before I say it. "You can tell me," he coaxes.

"I want—" I say, my voice soft and unsteady. He runs his fingers down the edge of my hairline, starting at my temple. It's so gentle, and that's not... exactly what I want. He waits patiently, brushing his rough fingertips down the side of my neck now, his eyes following the trail. "I want you to be in control," I say quietly. His eyes snap back to mine and narrow. "I want you to tell me what to do"—my cheeks are hot—"and I want you to make me do it." I bite my lip, hard. Perhaps the pain will distract me from the embarrassment of what I've just shared with him. I only manage to hold his gaze for a half second before I look to the side. My chest rises and falls beneath him, waiting.

I'm only held in suspense for a minute before his hand cups my jaw and turns my face. "Charlotte." His voice is rough and low. "Look at me." I do. I *want* to do as he asks, as I've just revealed.

"I would *love* to take control of you." There's a fervent look in his eyes, and a smirk on his lips, which softens for a moment with what he says next. He rubs his thumb along my lower lip as I soak everything in... I can't remember the last time I felt this vulnerable. "More than that," he says, "I'd be honored for you to give me the trust that requires." Something inside me begins to break open with that statement. I didn't realize how tightly wound I've been until this moment. I take a deep breath and shudder slightly upon exhale. His devilish grin returns, and he whispers in my ear, "And I was hoping you'd say that."

I tremble and adrenaline begins to course through me at a faster rate. We are no longer at a precipice. Things have tipped. Suddenly, Devo shifts his weight so that both of his hands are free. I don't want him to pull away after the intensity of our exchanged comments and my eyebrows draw down. Devo sees my expression and laughs with that warm tenor that I've begun to recognize.

"Oh, don't worry, love. We're just getting started."

"Ready when you are." I roll my eyes; cheekier than I intended to be.

"Ooo, a touch of sass." He gets off the couch, towering over me as I lay there. "And here I was thinking you'd be as sweet as your southern roots." I go to sit up and he puts up a finger. "Nuh uh, you're to stay where you are." I cock my head and my heart keeps racing as I recognize that we're working our way into a dynamic. A dynamic I want, but one I'm nervous about, and equally as excited for.

"Have you ever done something like this before?" he probes.

I glance left and right. "What do you mean? Hooking up with someone?"

He suppresses a smile and then schools his features into a serious mask. "No. I mean have you ever played with *control?*"

I shake my head and blink. He nods in response, looking away for a moment.

"Now this is important, Charlotte." He turns back to me and lowers himself down on one knee beside the couch. I twist my head to look him directly in the eyes.

I nod. "I'm listening."

"'Red' means stop. If you say 'red,' I will immediately stop whatever we're doing, no questions asked. Do you understand?"

I nod gravely, I think I know the rest of what he's about to say.

"'Yellow'—" he begins before I interrupt.

"You'll slow down," I finish, my voice quiet but sure. "Right?"

Devo cocks his head. "Yes, it does. Smart girl. And we will adjust what we are doing." I nod again in acquiescence.

"Would you like to guess what 'green' means?"

"I do have a driver's license, you know"—I roll my eyes—"I understand the meaning of a stoplight."

Devo raises his eyebrows but doesn't look displeased. In fact, it looks like he's preparing for a challenge as he tilts his chin up to look down at me. He then rubs his first two fingers along his bottom lip and shakes his head back and forth in thought. I imagine he's rifling through options, and I'm absolutely titillated.

"So, you know how to follow the rules of the road then, Miss Faure?"

I feel we just established this, so I simply nod—confused where this is going.

"Hmm." He inclines his head. "Well then, how did the last two nights of not touching yourself go?"

He can't possibly know how I would have reacted to that suggestion, could he? We hadn't had any kind of conversation about rule following or control before that. I think I'm hiding my thoughts, but once again, it appears Devo is reading me more than I would like.

"Charlotte"—he hangs on the last syllable—"I thought you liked following directions." His eyes rove my face. The truth of my morning activities must be written all over me.

"You said to hold off for the *night*." I tilt my chin up with feigned defiance. "And I did. For *both* nights." Another head cock from Devo, waiting for more.

My cheeks redden in anticipation of his reaction. "But you said nothing about this morning."

Devo laughs again and I feel my lips turning down in a scowl. I'm not sure what his laughter means and I'm ready to be defensive.

"Oh you beautiful, lustful, naughty young lady." He tsks and I squirm. "You know, I like the way you dressed today. I especially like this—" he fingers the soft yellow and white kerchief at my neck. In a few seconds, he has the knot undone and is pulling the fabric out from around my neck in a *whoosh*. He whips it up above my head and I lean back to see him threading my kerchief through the intricate back of the settee. Thick wooden flowers are carved into the wood with some gaps clear through to the other side.

"Give me your hands," he says gruffly. I slowly offer my hands to him, piecing together what he's going to do and wanting to follow instructions. He snags my wrists in one hand and pulls them up above my head. I feel the fabric wrap my wrists and go snug. Now I gasp aloud.

I look up at my wrists as best I can and give a few tugs. There's very little give. I'm simultaneously impressed by how fast Devo bound me, terrified, and, well, more than a little turned on. Devo watches me struggle for a moment before interrupting. "You're just tightening the knot, Charlotte," he says in a low voice with a smug look—his features dancing with playful tension.

From under the settee, Devo pulls out a matching red velvet pillow and places it in the gap between my back and the couch now that my wrists are pulling my body back and up. It was weirdly thoughtful. I shift to get more comfortable.

He drags his eyes up and down the full length of my body now and I shift again under his gaze. No, not shift. Writhe. The way my body moves on the couch is something out of my control. It's instinct, and I can tell that Devo's reacting on instinct too.

His jaw ticks as I lightly roll my hips, and his hands flex when I push up my breasts and allow my head to fall back slightly. Even though I'm the one tied down, I've ensnared the man standing free before me. Warmth rushes my chest and I feel pleased with myself. My alter ego is coming out and she demands to be thoroughly sexed.

"Now you just—" Devo manages to get out, gesturing at me with one of his palms "—stay like that." He slides his other hand down his face, as if he's trying to rid himself of a trance. "Just like that." He soaks me in for another long moment before he forces himself to turn on his heel and duck around the corner of the space. I thought I could see everything in here when I first walked in, but I realize there are a few nooks and crannies I hadn't been able to see around initially.

While Devo is out of my sight, a shred of doubt slips into my mind, and my sensual smile begins to fade. I trust Devo not to hurt me, and... I do believe he is who he says he is, but am I being too vulnerable with a near stranger?

Before this train of thought gets too far out of the station, Devo reappears from around the corner. Four red solo cups, unstacked, are clutched in one of his hands and paint brushes are in the other. He's already eyeing me again like I'm the most mesmerizing object he's ever seen. I feel admired. I imagine this is how a work of art feels.

"You tied me down to throw a frat party?" I nod my chin at the red cups held together by his long fingers.

"No, I tied you down because we can't have you touching yourself again, now can we?" He sets the solo cups down on the ground next to the elevated canvas.

My cheeks heat. "And because you wanted me to," he finishes with a wink. Before I can conjure a counterargument, he takes the three steps back to the settee to tower over me.

I'd just started to splutter out, "But we hadn't—I didn't—" when he puts his finger to my lips.

"I wanted to also, don't you worry." He runs his rough palm down the side of my face, my neck, my collar bone, and finally, *finally*, runs his hand over my breast. I can feel my nipple hardening and the fine hair on my arms raise. He continues down to my upper thigh and he squeezes, biting his lip. "In fact, I'd like to bind you in more ways." He grins down at me, and I realize I'm not alone in operating through a lustful haze. "I'd like to do all sorts of unspeakable things to you." He begins to slip up the hem of my shirt and he bends over to touch his lips to my lower abdomen, right above the button of my pants. Once again, the warmth of his breath against my skin has me aching. This man knows how to draw things out! We haven't even had a proper kiss yet, but my hips undulate at the graze of his full lips.

He sits up again quickly, removing himself from me, yet again. I yank against my wrist tie. "*Devo*," I let out in a half moan, half complaint.

"Oh, I know, believe me." Something in Devo's tightly controlled tone has my eyes flitting down to his pants. He's wearing black jeans, and now that I'm looking, I can see a bulge straining at his fly. I suck in a cheek and let my tongue wander around the inside of my mouth. Then I bite my lip at the realization of what I'm doing and try to stop my imagination from sucking a dick I hadn't yet seen. I am truly lost in this haze. At least it's not just me.

"And to answer your earlier question," he says, smiling over me, "the solo cups are not an indication of a frat party, missy. They are very important art supplies. The means to create are more accessible than people think." He says the last part under his breath. I mentally note the sentiment, but I have more important topics at hand.

"So where does this go, Devo?" I say from my post on the settee. "Do you paint me like one of your French girls?" I shift sideways, pointing my toes and arching my back—my version of a mock-sexy pose while in my current predicament. I pucker my lips for good measure.

He chuckles again and the corner of his lip tugs up. "Something like that," he murmurs, looking back and forth between me and the contents of the red solo cups. "And it's actually '*draw me* like one of your French girls' for your information. Common misconception," he chastises.

I roll my eyes and bite down on a smile.

"And what's a common misconception about you, then?" I tease.

"Hmm—" I can tell his mind is only half on the question. "—that as a man, I don't enjoy romance." He rolls his "r," making light of his answer, and I shock myself when a giggle escapes my lips. Our eyes meet and a shared grin spreads across our faces, like we're middle schoolers who've just cracked a stupid joke that landed with the class.

"Ah, yes," I say, "I've never been in such a romantic predicament." I glance up at my wrists, still smiling.

"Romance is in the eye of the beholder, Charlotte," he sing-songs.

"I thought that was beauty," I reply. "And art?"

"You don't think romance is an art?"

"Clearly, I don't know what constitutes art," I say, pointedly looking around.

His response is just a grin, albeit a charming one, but then his attention returns to his supplies.

After some consideration, he picks up one of the solo cups and uses it to pour what looks like white paint into another. He then stirs the concoction with a jumbo craft stick—something I recognize as a tool to mix paint.

I think back through all my research of Devo's past Muse Paintings. Many of them had been done in splattered jewel tones: royal blues and fire engine reds. The first one I'd ever seen had predominantly been a mixture of black splatters and an almost neon green as an accent.

"Starting already?" I ask, wanting as much of his attention as he'll give me.

"Mmm, yes we have." His tone is rich, and he casts me an admiring glance.

"How am I to collaborate like this then?" I tug at my wrists and raise an eyebrow.

"Oh, don't worry, you've already given me plenty to work with," he says, and then takes a cup and a brush over to the side of the raised canvas. Without much warning, Devo dips his brush in, raises his arm above his head and forcefully throws the paint down onto the canvas. My instinctual reaction is to pull back into the settee, even though the flying paint went nowhere near me, and in fact, didn't make it far past the canvas tarp beneath it. There are a few wayward flicks of light blue paint on the concrete floor opposite Devo now... but hey, it's an art studio closet, the flecks of paint blend right in.

I hear another splatter across the canvas and then Devo begins to move a bit quicker. He walks around the raised platform spraying the paint with throws and flicks of his arm and wrist. Sometimes the sound is loud and wet, sometimes it's a soft swish, like the sound of walking an umbrella between awnings in the rain.

I watch, mesmerized at how quickly he's working. I can't quite see the top of the canvas from my position since it's elevated a few inches above me. All I can see is the color and the tail of the splatters that miss the canvas. Could he possibly be painting a silhouette on there like this? Assuming that's what we're doing here.

Devo pauses to survey the results. His eyes drag down the canvas. My interest in him is no longer just physical, I want to know about his process.

"Devo?" I beckon.

"Hmm?" He sets his brush into another cup and rolls up his sleeves now that they've somewhat unfurled. It takes a moment before his eyes leave the canvas, like he can't tear them away.

Once his eyes are back on me, that mischievous gleam returns to his eyes and a corner of his mouth tugs up.

"Are you done?" I ask softly, hoping he's not, but also wanting to set my expectations correctly.

"Am I done?" He chuckles and shakes his head back and forth. "Charlotte, we've barely begun!" He crouches down beside me and goes to put his paint-speckled hands on either side of my hips before hesitating. "Are these pants important to you?" He holds himself back and looks me in the eyes.

I suppress a grin. How can this young man be so many things? He's kind and creative and in control. My control, on the other hand, is slipping; I feel myself wanting to curl up in the palm of his dexterous hand. Now it's my turn to laugh and I jut my chin down towards the paint swipes already gracing my jeans.

"I'm an artist too, you know," I say back. "And I wore these clothes to the studio for a reason."

"Good," he says hungrily. Before I know it, Devo's fingers are roughly opening the button on my pants and pulling them down to mid-thigh. I gasp.

Finally.

I don't realize how much heat I've been harboring between my legs until the cool air hits me. I squeeze my thighs together and squirm. Devo's watching me with his lower lip between his teeth. His warm hands grip my hips, just over the band of my panties. I'd chosen a navy lace number... you know, just in case.

I wish I could touch him in return, but all I can do is slant my hips toward him. He begins to run his hands up my outer thighs and over my hips, meeting the hem of my shirt and sliding under it, squeezing the sides of my waist. I love it. In this moment, I realize I don't want these warm, admiring hands to ever leave me. Part of me remembers that there was something else I cared about just seconds ago... what was it? *Oh!*

"So, um," I breathe, "why, um—" *Focus!* A little yelp escapes me as one of his hands slides down over the crotch of my underwear and cups me, his palm grinding slightly into my clit. "Why blue?"

"Why blue?" he murmurs into my neck, all whilst the heel of his hand rubs slow circles down below, and one moves up to clutch my breast.

"I've never seen you use a pastel like this before," I barely get out. His sensual movements pause, and he lets a couple seconds tick by before looking up at my face, his eyes sparkling.

"So, you've been looking me up, have you?" He's playful, if not a bit cocky. Of course I've looked him up and he knows it.

"The color is always inspired by the subject," he says, taking a moment to remove his hand from my breast and rub the scruff of his jaw. "And you have an innocence about you, but not a true naiveté." He glances at me, not sure how I'm going to take his explanation. "Just a softness, a femininity that's pure, like a gentle morning."

I listen, enrapt.

"I'm not as innocent as you seem to think," I challenge.

"Oh, I believe you." He shows me that wolfish grin. "It's more of the aura that you exude." Then he softens the smile. "And I saw your painting, the woman in the field with the—" he waves his hand in the air by his head.

"The mist," I say. "The woman in the mist." My volume drops

off. I'm surprised he brought up my work in progress, but it makes sense he stole a look when he left the note on my easel.

"I may have taken inspiration from the hues there," he says. A warmth spreads throughout my chest.

"So what's on the canvas now?" I ask. He looks over at where it lays from my vantage point.

"Ah, yes, you can't see from here." He smiles, then bends over my abdomen, beginning to kiss my stomach. His lips graze over the top of my belly button, and head lower. "That's just the background," he breathes across my skin. "We have yet to paint the subject." He looks up at me and winks, then slides a corner of my underwear down and exposes skin that never sees the sunlight. I want him with an animalistic need at this point—I urge my hips up.

He pushes me back down. "Nuh-uh. I'm in charge, Charlotte." I groan in response.

He keeps going, one slow lap with his tongue of the area just above my clit. A sharp intake of breath from me. Then a lazy lap *around* my clit. My eyes almost roll back in my head. At this point, I'm a simple vessel of need and my body is acting accordingly.

Finally, he hooks both sides of my underwear with his forefingers and begins to pull them down to the bottom of my thighs. He does so at an excruciatingly slow pace. With my pants and underwear still bunched around my knees, my thighs are pressed together. Devo takes one hand and slides his fingertips down my slit between my inner thighs. His calloused fingers against the wet heat of my folds is everything I want in that moment. More. I want more. I want to place his hand back over me, but I'm once again reminded that I'm restricted.

He brings his fingers to his mouth then and sucks off my wetness, looking directly in my eyes as he does so. Once he's done, he grins and licks his lips. It's the sexiest thing I've ever seen.

"Damn," I breathe, eyelids heavy. The physical ache in my

wrists and arms is completely overcome by the needy ache weighing heavy on all my erogenous zones.

"I love the way you taste," Devo semi-growls. He's staring at the fresh pearlescence gleaming between my thighs and I can see the yearning. Devo tugs my jeans and underwear further down and pulls them off over my feet. I do anything I can to help so I point my toes. It's both liberating and frustrating to be so physically limited. I'm trusting this man to do what he wants with me in a way that satisfies both of us, and it's exhilarating.

Devo notices my ballerina toes and the corner of his mouth tugs up. Thank goodness Mariah and I had gotten pedicures just a few days ago. My toes are painted with a soft baby blue polish. He grabs the arch of my foot with one hand and murmurs, "Looks like I picked the right color for you, Miss Faure."

"Beginner's luck," I retort, but it comes out slow and sticky. The blood coursing through me has been heavily re-routed from my brain to areas that only seek physical pleasure. He arches an eyebrow after planting a soft kiss on the top of my foot. Then he begins to slide his hands up my leg. I shiver. I'd never shared a sensual experience with someone that was this drawn out. Not even with myself.

"Oh, I'm no beginner," he replies. Devo's hand stops at my lower thigh and suddenly, he's lifted my nearest leg up over his head and draped it across his outer shoulder. His head is now between my legs as he kneels on the ground. He tugs my body so it's at a more convenient angle for what he's about to do next. I bite my lip in anticipation.

"A beginner with you maybe," he continues, "but let's see if we can't graduate to the next level." With that, Devo places his head right in front of my pussy and gives a long, luxurious lick up my slit. My abdomen muscles tense and I let out a moan. His multi-colored eyes look up at me from between my legs and pin me to the settee. I amend what I had previously said to myself. *This* is the sexiest thing I have ever seen.

Devo flashes me a knowing grin then puts his tongue to

further use. A few more long, slow licks are followed up with more targeted movements. He swirls his tongue around my clit now and I involuntarily jerk—I'm so swollen and sensitive, every circle has my eyes rolling into the back of my head.

The more my body twitches, the more aggressive Devo's grip becomes on my thighs. I love it. I love the feeling of his strong hands holding me down to him, keeping his mouth to me. My moans begin to grow louder, and needier. I roll my hips as much as I can from this position, attempting to ride his mouth. It's instinct. Whenever he works his way faster in a pattern, I can feel my thigh muscles start to spasm, and they attempt to clench shut. Devo's hands keep prying my legs back open to allow his head more movement. When he does so, my moans develop into louder vocalizations. I don't even know what sounds are crossing my lips.

Every few moments, I cast a glance back down towards him; each time, I catch his piercingly pale-eyed stare, hungrily soaking in my reactions. That sight, combined with the physical sensations, is almost too much to bear.

Through it all, I ache for more—for this man to be inside of me. It's as if he reads my mind. The hand that had been holding my thigh closest to the back of the settee is suddenly gone. And then I feel it. A warm fingertip at my entrance.

"Ah, yesss," I let out, wishing I could inch my pelvis forward.

Devo stops his licking and sucking for a moment and hovers above me. "Is this what you want?"

"Yes, yes," I squirm. His lips curve into a devilish smile, and he allows his finger to penetrate me deeper. I bite my lip. Everything is a build with this man. Suddenly, I can feel my entrance stretched just a bit wider, and I realize he's inserted a second finger. I release a shaky breath.

"Please!" I drop my head back, not sure how much teasing I can endure at this stage.

Devo makes an affirmative sound with his throat and then curls his two fingers inside of me to press against that sensitive ridged spot. He swivels the heel of his hand slightly to suck on my clit at the same moment and my hips buck. He takes his other hand off the thigh that's draped over his shoulder and uses his forearm to brace my hips down against the velvet settee.

"Downn, girl." He laughs again and then twists his two fingers inside of me, giving my clit another swirl of his tongue. I emit a desperate shriek. But his arm bar works. I open my eyes just in time to see his muscles relax after straining to prevent my hips from rising off the couch.

"Do you want more?"

"Yes, please," I whimper.

"Ok then, Miss Faure," he says in a husky voice. So many thoughts and questions swirl through my head but none make purchase in my lustful haze. I'm a wet, swollen, desperate mess and I stare into his eyes as if he were the only thing I've ever wanted.

"I have a task for you," he says. I nod, thinking I want whatever's on the other side of this bargain. "I would like to go back to eating you out—"

"And you'll use your fingers?" I plead.

His eyes sparkle at my clear desire. "Yes, I'll use my fingers." To demonstrate, he plunges the two already inside of me even deeper and I gasp.

"But if you want me to bring you back to the edge, I want to see if you can do something for me in return," he continues.

"Yes, yes," I say, wiggling my toes in anticipation. "Wait, what is it?" I tip my head up to look at him more fully.

"I need you to be silent," he says. "No sound can escape your lips." He brings the pointer finger of his free hand up to my lips in the universal shushing sign. I hesitate for a moment before trying to suck the tip of his finger into my mouth. He pulls it away and chuckles again.

"Nuh uh, your mouth isn't being used right now." I pout in response.

"I'm sorry if I was, uh, making too much noise," I say. Why

does he want me to be quiet? Why am I apologizing? I thought he'd emptied the place for this very reason.

"No, Charlotte, I love how you sound"—he removes his fingers to lap up my cunt again—"and how you taste." He licks his lips and fingers. I love the warmth of his tongue but I'm missing the penetration. I want him to fill me. To fuck me. "This request is because I want to see if you can do what I say. No noise, okay?"

"Okay," I say breathlessly. "Yes, I'll be quiet."

He shows off a full grin now. "Good girl," he growls and quickly lowers his head again—he doesn't see my eyes go wide. *Good girl.* Good girl? It sounded patronizing, it sounded like the creation of some sort of hierarchy between us. It sounded... *it sounded...* it sounded delicious. I liked it. Laying before Devo, in this moment, I'm like a delicate piece of chocolate placed too close to the burner. This man has begun to melt me. I am willing and pliable in his hands. I submit to him.

As Devo continues to pleasure me, I keep my mouth closed when I can. And when I can't, I keep my shuddering inhales and exhales as soundless as possible.

Devo's added a third finger inside of me, and I can feel myself being filled and stretched further as he begins to use those fingers to thrust into me over and over. This, combined with his talented tongue, has me seeing stars. My muscles start their tremors. One of those tremors sends the thigh that was resting on his shoulder sliding down. Without missing a beat, he uses his free hand to lift my leg back up, hitching it back up on his shoulder and holding it there.

My thighs suddenly clamp shut, squeezing his head to me. He doesn't slow down. My back arches violently and I desperately want to scream. But instead, the phrase *good girl, good girl,* keeps floating through my head. I want to be a good girl. I want to deserve this. I can feel my calf on the verge of cramping, while at the same time, that magical tingling sensation kicks off in my lower abdomen. It's happening. I turn my head into my upper arm, still hoisted above my head, and bite my skin to stifle any sound that might escape.

I careen over the edge.

My whole body pulses with a rhythm emanating from where Devo had done the lord's work. He continues his licking and thrusting through it all, but slower, letting me ride it out. Finally, the spasms subside and Devo takes both hands and wraps them around my thighs to pry them away from his head. He comes up for air to look at me—he sports a knowing grin, and his lips shine.

"How was that?" he asks.

I feel like I've simultaneously been knocked out and am floating. I smile lazily and open my mouth to respond, but then snap it shut. Is this a trick question? Can I speak now? I'm not currently at peak cognitive ability and I don't want to break any rules.

"You don't have to be silent anymore." Devo laughs as he wipes his mouth with the back of his hand. He gently lifts my leg off his shoulder, up over his head and sets it back down on the couch. Thank goodness too, because I don't think I can navigate the movements of my limbs gracefully at the moment.

"That was amazing," I say from my cotton candy cloud.

Devo laughs and kisses the top of my thigh.

"I didn't make a sound!" I suddenly exclaim, as if sharing my straight-A report card.

Another amused rumble from Devo. "Yes, you did a good job."

Devo then stands and leans over me. I realize in that moment that he's still fully clothed, as I've been laying before him, pantless. He kisses my forehead and then goes to work on the knot keeping my wrists bound to the wooden carving of the settee. When they're released, Devo does the same to my arms as he did to my leg and gently moves my limbs from their stressed position and into my lap. He rubs my wrists in a massage-like motion for a few moments before standing up again to assess me.

My fingertips are tingling, partially from being over my head, but also because my intense arousal had drawn the blood away from my extremities.

I still feel like I'm floating as Devo delicately slides my underwear back up my legs. When he can scoot them up no further, he helps me to stand and then pulls my panties up all the way. My lace underwear looks so fragile in his larger masculine fingers. Devo then clasps the hem of my T-shirt. "May I take this off?" I nod in silence and raise my arms above my head, fingers still tingling. He pulls it up over my head and places it on the couch. Now I'm standing in my bra and panties, both made with navy lace designs. I guess an effort to pick a matching set didn't go to waste after all.

"And this?" He gestures to my bra. I acquiesce again, and he steps in close, wrapping his arms around to my back. My nose is nearly pressed against his chest and I smell his musky scent once again. This close, however, I also catch the scent of the sweat that's gleaming at the hollow of his neck. And I catch a whiff of... *sex*. He smells like sex.

I stand there in his partial embrace while his nimble fingers unhook my bra. He slides the fabric down over my arms and fingertips, then he tosses it on the couch as well.

"Why?" I shake my head back and forth, trying to clear the endorphin fog. The cool air hits my chest and my nipples peak ever so slightly. I don't look down. *Now's not the time to be self-conscious*, I think. That moment has passed.

"Just trust me," he says against my ear, his voice gravelly. I realize that I've had a release and Devo likely hasn't. He glances down at my breasts and his eyes harden. While we're still so close, I twist my palm to feel for his crotch. His dick is straining at his fly, hard and full. He shakes his head back and forth on the side of my head, kissing the shell of my ear and removing my hand from his fly.

"Not right now," he murmurs. My eyebrows draw down.

"But I want you to feel good too."

"Don't worry, I feel great," he says, wiping a wayward strand of hair from my forehead, slicked down with perspiration. Without warning, Devo stoops down and sweeps me up into his arms, one arm under my legs and the other below my shoulder blades.

"Where are we going?" I almost slur. I sound like a drunk! Devo turns and takes the few steps to the platform with the canvas atop it. He walks up the one step of the platform and gingerly places me on my side at the center of the platform's plateau. I still feel like putty and stay exactly as he's placed me. The light blue paint must be smearing beneath me and a part of me recognizes that we've moved back into art. I don't want to ruin his process.

"Charlotte—" He clears his throat as he stands over me. "I want you to remember how you felt just a moment ago." He's focusing on me with an electric energy, but his voice remains strained.

That shouldn't be too hard because I'm still flush with feel-good hormones. I give him a small nod, knowing my movements can smear the paint and not sure what my new rules are.

"You can move." He gives me a soft smile. "I just need your essence on the canvas." *My essence.* "I'll handle the details."

"Okay," I respond, now feeling shy. This is how I'm collaborating. I'm one foot in my endorphin high, chemical-driven, lustful haze, and one foot in a puddle of returning nerves. I close my eyes and try to imagine the peak of my orgasm just a couple minutes ago. I begin to arch my back more and slightly lengthen my legs, still keeping them somewhat bent. I point my toes, almost re-triggering the cramp I'd been close to. I smile slightly. How silly it feels to cramp amidst such pleasure.

Something's still missing. I look up at Devo and he gives a nod of his chin, indicating permission to do whatever I need to. I slide my arm out from under me and put both of my arms above my head, my hands hanging above the canvas, wrists touching. There we go. That feels more like how I'd felt moments ago. Devo smiles conspiratorially. He walks over to my hands hanging off the canvas and grasps my wrists with a warm, firm grip. I use that to anchor me as I fully arch my back and tilt my head up.

"Perfect," he says and lets go of my wrists. "Stay like this." I can feel him splaying my hair out behind me onto the canvas.

"Don't worry." His voice is husky. "The paint comes out." I wasn't even thinking about my hair, maybe I should have been.

I focus on maintaining the last remnants of my high. *Good girl,* I go over again. I think about Devo tying my wrists, restraining me. I bite my lip. I think about his piercing gaze over my clit as he gave me wave after wave of pleasure. I can feel my pussy begin to pulse again, just thinking about it. I let out a sigh of wistful rapture.

"There," Devo commands. "Stay there." His voice fades out for a moment and then he's back: "Close your eyes and mouth, please."

I do as I'm told. I can't see what's happening, but I can feel it. Swaths of paint are splattered across my body from all sides. I hold my position. Just like before, some of the splatters feel and sound larger, lightly stinging my mostly naked body. Other sprays are light and ticklish, causing shivers to skitter across my skin.

I wish I could experience Devo's point of view, but I'm soaking up every moment of being a part of it. The pleasure of my orgasm has almost faded, but it's been replaced by the pleasure of being admired, of being a part of a creation, of being a *muse.*

Chilly splatters wash across my stomach, the tops of my feet, my lower back. I arch slightly further. What would it feel like for other people to watch this process? That thought kind of turns me on... I like the idea of being a work of art.

The splatters become fewer and farther between. I can imagine Devo is focusing on the details now as best he can while

I'm still on the canvas, memorizing my shape with the paint. Finally, it stops. A contemplative silence hangs in the air.

"You can open your eyes."

I do. I see dashes of a soft green paint before me. Devo had somehow avoided harsh splatters across my face. I look towards the edge of the canvas and see a deep black paint dripping off the edge. I hadn't realized that he'd switched colors. The juxtaposition of the soft blues and greens with the deep black is harsh, indicative of tension.

"How did it go?" I ask, looking up at him.

"Well," he answers with a warm smile. He wipes his brow with his forearm. "Really well." He bends down to kiss my head again. It's sweet and gentle. I warm to him in a different way. Devo has brought me through so many stages this afternoon.

He helps me stand, minimizing additional points of contact with the canvas. Once he assists me down the platform step, Devo embraces me in a tight hug. He kisses my temple. God, I love the tender kisses he's given me throughout the night. This man brought me to the moon with his tongue and talented fingers, and then has me melting before him with the softest brush of his lips.

"Thank you," he rasps. He pulls my head up to his, finger under my chin. "Thank you. You're beautiful Charlotte, absolutely gorgeous."

I smile up at him, not sure what to say. "You're welcome?" I laugh and bite my lower lip. I shift my weight from foot to foot and give him a once over. "Would you like me to?" I pointedly eye his straining fly then look back into his eyes.

He shakes his head. "No, no, don't worry about that," he drawls.

"You sure?" My eyebrows knit together. I know how frustrated I was not long ago feeling so swollen and turned on before reaching a release. He puts his forehead to mine and nods softly. Our close eye contact feels intimate.

"I'm sure." He takes a deep breath and draws back. He pulls a clean hand towel seemingly out of nowhere and gently wipes as much paint as he can off my body. "Now this is my least favorite part. I have to finish this"—he gestures over his shoulder at the canvas—"and clean up. And you, missy—" he runs his rough fingertips down my now paint-splattered arm "—need to clean yourself up." I shiver, but begin to slide my bra back on. Devo bends down and comes up with my T-shirt, which he gently pulls down over my head. I frown as I poke my arms through the sleeves. I don't want to leave.

"Can we be together for a moment?" I ask shyly. "Just for a bit?"

"Yes, of course," he says. "Whatever you need." He kisses my cheek and scoops me up again. I emit a squeak of surprise and then giggle, wrapping my hands around his neck. I know it's just the chemicals coursing through me, but I *feel* something towards this man. It's as if I'm basking in his warmth, and if I'm near him I'm safe. I feel sexy. I'm content.

Devo sweeps us out of the closet-turned-sexy-art-room and walks us through the empty studio. We round into the small alcove that is the kitchen. He sets me on the counter after throwing a clean smock down to prevent my bare skin from touching the cold countertop.

"I hope you have laundry services here." He smiles as he fills a glass of water and hands it to me. "Since you're such a *dirty* girl and all." He eyes the smock beneath me and waggles his eyebrows.

I lightly smack him on the arm and laugh. "Hey, I was perfectly innocent when I came here."

"Sure you were," he parries, snagging my hand and bringing it to his lips. "And you just thought I was an innocent landscape painter." He nips at my fingertips and I yelp.

"Hey! I didn't know what was going to happen in there," I say indignantly, grinning.

"Hmm, you're not complaining now, are you?"

I look away from him and sip my water; I have no come

back. "No," I mumble, "I'm not complaining." I try to stifle the smile that wants to spread across my lips. No, I'm not going to complain about having one of the best orgasms of my life and then becoming a work of art. I steal a glance back at Devo and he's grinning with a pointed look in his eye. Fine, he knows what he's doing. Speaking of...

"Hey," I begin in a less flirtatious tone, "is this how all of your Muse Paintings, um, happen?" A blush creeps up my cheeks. I don't really want to ask him about other women he's been with but... this is what he's known for, isn't it?

Devo tips his head sheepishly. "Everyone's different..." He splays his hands out—I can see him thinking how best to explain. Then he looks me in the eye and rubs the back of his head with a hand, probably spreading paint through his hair. "But yes, I do my best work with real inspiration."

I nod repeatedly, looking around and swinging my legs. Now that I know what he's like, I want Devo just for myself, but I figured as much. Warm hands come up to cup my cheeks and I look up into his imploring stare.

"But hey," he says softly, "to be honest, I don't always have a connection with someone like this." He gestures between us.

I look up at him through my lashes. "Thank you," I whisper. I don't quite know what I'm saying thank you for. Perhaps it's for the acknowledgement that he actually likes me as a person, and not just as a body. Or perhaps it's for giving me this entire experience, for allowing me to create something with him. Or perhaps I'm even saying thank you for getting me off, or getting me water, or giving me comfort when I need it. I don't know why I said it, but I meant it.

"No, Charlotte"—he smiles softly—"thank *you*." With that, he helps me down off the counter and waits for me as I pad off to the restroom. I come out to see him putting his ancient phone in his back pocket as he holds out his other hand, which I clasp. We swing our joined hands on our jaunt back through the studio. Once back in the converted closet, we plop down on the settee again and I drape my legs over his, just like how we started. He lands soft kisses across my cheeks, and I return a few, although they make me feel shy. Which is hilarious considering everything we just did together.

He puts his hand to my cheek, and I feel his thumb brush my dimple. It reminds me of our pen pal exchanges and how far we've come. His faint smile makes me think that he's remembering it too. All those postscripts and all our banter. My bad jokes and his mysterious alter-egos.

Speaking of... "Hey, Devo, er, Devlin?" I hesitate. "What do you want me to call you?"

"You can call me whatever you want now, Miss *Charlotte G. Faure.*" I give him a pointed look at the use of my full name, but deep down, I'm impressed he remembers my middle initial from my very first tipsy email.

He just shrugs and smiles.

"So... Devlin," I start, "who was I sending all those letters to for all those weeks? There was a Mark R. and a Sam G."—I look up at the ceiling—"I know there were others, but I can't remember."

He puts his arm around me and kisses the top of my shoulder. "Those were all me." He gives me a soft squeeze before releasing me. "I just like to use additional pseudonyms while travelling. I use the names of my favorite abstract painters. Mark Rothco and Sam Gilliam... I would've used Jackson P., but I thought that might be too obvious." He displays a cheeky grin and I playfully push against his bicep.

"Okay so you like to confuse people?" I narrow my eyes, partly teasing.

"I... like to be more anonymous than not," he admits. "But also, I like the mystery. What's life without a little bit of intrigue??" He beams as he tips his forehead toward me, and I can tell he means it. A man of intrigue he is, then! Good to know.

I ask him a few more questions about his travels, his paintings, his plans. He tells me he's an early riser, and I groan while admitting that I'm a night owl. I find out he has an older brother and that they were raised by their mom and her *three* sisters. We have more in common about our upbringings than I expected.

He deflects deeper questions and asks me about my journey to Brooklyn. I share a few of the wild one-liners Harper and her friend have doled out when I've helped them with their social media shoots. He shakes his head laughing and rolls his eyes with me.

"Humans are fascinating, aren't they?" he says to me. And I agree. Fascinating and terrible and sometimes tantalizing, everything all at once.

He shares his surprise at the success of the Muse series and alludes to the luck he had with his first piece. I think he's referring to the Mischa painting, due to its virality... but I'm not one hundred percent sure. His eyes glaze over for a moment when he mentions it, and I can tell there's a depth of feeling there that he's trying to pass over. My nosy (and a bit jealous) side wants to ask more questions, but I bite my tongue. Despite all his optimism and positivity and joie de vivre, I pick up on a thread of cynicism when he discusses the art world, or even society at large.

"It's everything, you know." He smiles sideways at me, one arm draped over my shoulders, holding me close and keeping me warm. "Art drives humanity forward, while also documenting our experience, inspiring it." I can feel his tense passion vibrating just beneath the skin. I'm certain he can make a full speech on the subject. He continues, "But very few people are able to make the time for it nowadays, much less make money from it, or allocate *to* it." He trails off and sits back to stare across the room, over the canvas we'd just worked on together. "And unfortunately, you do run into some shady characters in this world."

I chew on that—hoping he isn't one of them.

"Earlier you mentioned your fifteen minutes of fame," I begin, wanting to understand him. He turns to look at me expectantly, waiting for a question. "I know, um"—I bite my lip—"I mean, I've *seen* that there are a lot of beautiful women out there who would pay you to paint them"—I hesitate—"like this." I sweep my arm toward the canvas. His eyes dance.

"*You* are a beautiful woman, Charlotte," he says softly. "What's your question?"

I try to contain my shy smile. "I mean surely there are more beautiful, and *famous* women who would pay you *a lot* of money to paint them." If Mischa speaks to her peers about him the same way she speaks in her Vogue interview, I have no doubt he had plenty of potential high-net worth clients. "Why are you doing what you're doing? Going around to amateur studios, spending time with normal people?"

"Normal people," he repeats and chuckles, shaking his head. "Well, yes I do think I'm in the middle of my fifteen minutes of fame." He rubs his chin. "And I thought maybe I could use it to help people, bring attention to regular studios around the country and unknown artists—get the public interested in their local art scene again." He smiles and takes his hand off my thigh to give a one-handed shrug. "It's the best idea I could think of to spread some of the success I'm having to others who deserve more attention for their work."

My heart squeezes. He could be making tens of thousands, or I don't know, hundreds of thousands of dollars running his Muse series through the rich and famous. Instead, he's trying to uplift visual art as a whole—to uplift people like me, and Alex and even Daisy, not that that was why she was interested in him at McArthur's.

Devo absentmindedly goes to run his palm down the back of my hair. His hand stops once it gets tangled in the paint-matted waves. He's shaken out of his reverie. "Charlotte—" His eyebrows draw together apologetically as he takes in my extra colorful appearance. "Unless you want this paint to be near-impossible to wash out, you should get in the shower."

My eyes widen. This paint better come off me! "Oh!" I exclaim. "I thought you said it washes out??"

"It does..." he says, but scrunches his nose.

His eyes home in on my discarded jeans. He gets up to collect them and hands them to me. "Don't worry, you have time, but"—he tilts his head to the side in concession—"it is extra tough to remove once it's fully dry."

"Oh gosh," I say, feeling the drying clumps in my hair.

"Come here." He opens his arms after I slide my pants up my legs and pop the button through the hole. I walk into his embrace one last time. He kisses the top of my head again and we rock back and forth in a tight embrace. "Thank you for today," he says above my head. "You were incredible, and it was an honor."

Why do I feel so emotional around this farewell? I glance at the drying paint, and I can just make out the outline of my body. It's nowhere near what a final Muse Painting looks like. He's got some work to do.

"Good luck." I jut my chin towards the canvas.

He lets me go and lightly knocks my chin with a knuckle. "I don't need it," he says. "You've already given me everything I could possibly need." I roll my eyes at him, but secretly, I'm flattered. I pull my phone out of my purse and bring up a ride-share app—there's no way I'm subwaying in this state. Devo places his hand over the screen, forcing me to look up at him.

"There's already a car outside for you," he says, "if you want it."

"What?" I say in disbelief.

"I had my assistant find someone willing to wait"—he shifts his feet—"while you were in the bathroom."

"Oh," I say, surprised. "Thank you." And I mean it. I feel taken care of, and it's... soothing. I could get used to this, but I know I shouldn't.

He gives a side smile and then spins me around and gives me a light slap on the ass.

"Hey!"

"Get a move on, Charlotte," he says as I playfully glare at him over my shoulder and move toward the door. "Leave the artist to his work! And save that beautiful hair of yours!"

I shake my head and laugh. "I wanted to buzz it off anyway," I shout back.

"Don't try me, I'll make you re-do the painting to match the new silhouette!" I skitter out of the room, shoes in one hand, purse in the other. Although... doing this all again doesn't sound like such a terrible idea.

On the ride home I realize I don't have my neck scarf. *Oh well*, I think. He can have a memento of me. I wish I had one of him.

Chapter Four
DAY AFTER

By the time I get home, it's dark and I'm exhausted. I get in a steaming hot shower and go over my hair and skin with multiple rounds of shampoo and soap. Once I'm fairly certain I've gotten out all of the blue, green and black flecks of paint, I cover my hair in record-breaking dollops of conditioner. I sit on the tiled floor and let the stream hit my back, leaning my head forward and out of the spray to allow the moisturizing concoction to soak in before I rinse one last time.

Once I'm done in the shower, I step out and towel off, then moisturize my skin with the same gusto. My paint-smudged grey T-shirt hangs from the towel rack. I thought maybe I'd throw it away, but now, I think I'll keep it. This can be *my* memento—my proof of this afternoon.

After downing a bowl of microwaveable easy mac while wrapped in my towel, I hastily brush my teeth and flop into bed. My phone buzzes with texts from people in my life I don't have the attention span for at the moment, including Mariah. She's spending the night at her fellow TA's apartment. He's cute! Good for her.

A piece of me wishes I could wait on a text from Devo, but of course we'd never exchanged numbers, only addresses. I pick up my phone to send a text to a thread of my closest girlfriends numerous times but always wind up deleting it. The intention of the NDA I signed earlier hangs over my head, but I *could* tell them I spent an afternoon with a man. A world-shattering afternoon with a beautiful, thoughtful, *skilled* man. I put my phone down and stare at the ceiling for a moment, wondering when I'll see him again—wondering if it'll only ever be in my dreams. Before I know it, I'm fast asleep.

The next day I wake up shaking my head at my dramatic thoughts from the night before. I'll definitely see Devo again—what was this? Romeo and Juliet? Was one of us planning to perish by poison? All I want to do is head back to the studio and peek in the closet I saw stars in last night to check on Devo's progress.

But first, my paying job.

Harper texted me early this morning asking if I could come over for a home shoot. She just adopted a puppy and wants to announce it to her followers. I hesitate before my closet and finally pick out a cream-colored maxi dress with pastel flowers printed across it, then throw a baby blue sweater over the dress and belt it at the small of my waist. I slide into my tawny brown leather boots with pointed toes that I feel give my legs some extra length. I'd be lying if I said I wasn't thinking about Devo's height and wanting to be closer to his full lips.

Yesterday, Devo saw me in a studio outfit because I'd expected to need to roll up my sleeves and get messy... which I did, but not in the way I'd anticipated. Today, I want to look more feminine. I dab on more make-up than normal and take extra time to weave a long, fishtail braid through my hair. When my fingers finally cease their movement, I scoff at myself. I'm dressing for a man I barely know! He clearly already enjoyed me in the state I was in yesterday and yet here I am, preening in the mirror—pretending he's right in front of me and wanting to catch his eye. I stop just before putting on eyeshadow and step away from my beauty station. This is good enough. I have to get moving before Harper returns the puppy to the pound.

Once at her parents' townhouse, I help Harper find the best lighting and set up a scene with the heartwarmingly adorable Great Dane puppy. He still has little grey fat rolls going down his body, and I just want to squeeze him 'til he pops.

"Duke, Duke." Harper pats a forest green, velvet pillow on the floor in front of her. It's rimmed with gold piping and has opulent tassels hanging from the corners: a pillow fit for royalty. The puppy ignores her and keeps licking my hand while I laugh. I scoot his butt back over toward the patch of natural light next to his owner, but we've lost both his attention and his interest in treats. The first few had kept him on the pillow, but now he's more fascinated by the new human creature crouched before him with a camera.

Harper sighs. "Okay, I guess that's all we're going to get today," she murmurs, smacking the pillow out of the way and standing up, brushing nonexistent dust off the skirt of her tight fuchsia dress. I allow Duke to give my hand a few more kisses before I pull away. As I do, I notice the tiniest speck of light blue on the back of my thumb. Must have overlooked that in the shower last night. Who knows what other stubborn spots I had missed?

An image of Devo's devilish grin and piercing gaze between my thighs flashes through my mind and I put my hand to my brow, riding out a tingling sensation in my lower abdomen.

"Do you want a drink?" Harper asks from behind the kitchen counter. She's pouring herself what looks like a glass of chilly white wine. "Owning a puppy is hard work!" she exclaims before taking what can only be described as a gulp.

I suppress a grin at the thought that Harper has only had Duke for two days. Pet ownership is going to be a long, bumpy road, but despite her occasional air of entitlement, Harper would never give him back to the shelter. She has a bigger heart than expected under those designer clothes, and would be more likely to put him up for adoption on her Instagram story than put him back in a cage. In the meantime, if he can hold her attention and she can manage his growth, Duke will be the luckiest little guy in all of Brooklyn.

"No that's okay," I finally answer. Harper is already halfway done with her glass. "I actually have somewhere to be." Harper's shoulders droop. I'd had the sense lately that she might want to... be friends. Not something I'd given much thought to, as I didn't want to risk my paycheck. Instead, I've been kind, polite and professional. I'm sure she has a pack of glamorous peers to hang out with anyway.

But just as I think this, I catch her eyeing a well-worn stack of flowery romance novels on an end table and realize, I really don't know how she spends her time outside of *influencing*.

"Alright then, well, I'll see you this weekend." She pulls her expression together, no longer looking put out. "We have a shoot with Christina." Another rising influencer in Williamsburg, best known for reviewing "see-and-be-seen" bars and restaurants. "Wait, what day is it again?" Her eyebrows knit together as she pours a second glass of wine.

"Today's Thursday." I gather up my belongings and don my coat.

"Right, okay." Harper waves me away. "I'll send you money for your time." She cocks her head. "You know, you look really pretty today, Char. Do you have a date tonight?" Her eyes light up.

"No, no, nothing special," I reply, ducking my head and tugging on my braid as I near the door.

"Ah ok, see you in a few days then," she shouts after me.

"See you in a few days!" I lean back across the threshold of the townhouse and yell again, "Bye Duke!" I spy him gnawing on the bottom of a heavy gray curtain—he almost blends in. I close the door to the sounds of: "Duke! Bad boy! Drop it!"

I head down the steps with a smile. I did not sign up for puppy training when I agreed to this job, so I better get the hell out of here. *It's Thursday*, I think. Devo's always revealed his Muse Paintings during these micro-residencies on Fridays. He must be working on it now. Even though I'm not in the headspace to paint, my feet take me in the direction of the Copper Works. I didn't do all that primping today for nothing.

When I enter the studio, it's late afternoon and the sun is streaming through the high western-facing windows. The place is bustling! Perhaps the temporary close of the studio yesterday had people antsy. Nearly everyone I know who's a member of Copper Works is in attendance. Alex is elbow deep in clay on the right, closer to the large basin sinks. Miles looks to be putting on more layers to his multi-media canvas. In fact, it looks like he's trying to attach pieces of a PVC pipe and he hasn't quite figured out the right adhesive. Daisy, true to her namesake, is actually painting flowers, but on torn cloth rather than a mounted canvas. I look up and see a few other pieces of jagged-edged cloth hanging from a rusted wire over her head, each end attached to two adjacent walls. Daisy's corner. Every strip has a plant painted on it. *Hmm, a hanging forest?* I also spot Rob waving wide strokes of slate blue watercolor across his handmade paper. His watercolor landscapes are always lovely, and I wonder what this one's inspired by.

After my quick assessment of the activity in the space, my eyes zero in on the closet door. The portal to Devo's temporary mini studio, *or sex den*. I purse my lips to hide my smile. No one's given me a second glance. So, despite the secret blaring through my mind, I casually stroll towards that closet. I expect someone to see me and stop me, especially Alex, who I assume Devo worked with to coordinate the empty studio yesterday, but no one says a thing.

My heart rate starts rising as I approach the door. I take a deep breath and put my hand on the knob, then retract it. I look around one more time to confirm no one is paying attention to me, and then give two raps against the wood with my right knuckles. I'm hoping everyone's distracted from the fact that I'm knocking on a *closet door*. Nothing happens. So, I turn the knob and open.

A small part of me is expecting, and hoping, to see Devo in here, his attention fully enrapt with the outline of my silhouette. The thought gives me a pleasant buzz. But a more realistic part of me expects to at least see a drying canvas in the room, even if no one is presiding over it. I'm wrong, on both counts. I drop my hand from the doorknob and let it hit the side of my thigh. I frown as my eyes frantically search the space.

The closet is full. Bursting, in fact, with art supplies. There are cans of paint stacked to my left, a stockpile of brushes beside it. New and old canvases are leaning against the right wall. I see a set of rolling metal shelves against the back wall with stacks of pottery equipment and boxes full of odds and ends. There's also a yellow janitor's cart with a mop sticking out of it, the wooden end leaning against the drab concrete wall.

What?

Where's the settee and the Persian rug? The very large, very wet painting that had been here a mere 24 hours ago? Maybe I'd expected the champagne bucket to be gone... but all the furniture? The art? The artist? Where was he?

Again, he's never here when I expect him to be. Devo comes and goes as he pleases and that both intrigues and frustrates me. I shut the door, careful not to make any loud noises, and go to turn on my heel when a male voice makes me jump.

"Looking for your boy?" Alex is awkwardly hanging right behind me, clay covering his fingers and wrists and streaked across the front of his smock. I put my hand over my heart.

"Jesus, Alex, you scared the shit out of me," I say back, trying to calm my pulse and looking behind him to see if I have anyone else's attention. I don't.

"Sorry"—he grimaces—"I only noticed you in here when you were halfway across the room."

"It's okay"—I wave at the air and shake my head, allowing a little laugh on my exhale—"I just didn't expect someone to be *right behind me.*" I give him a pointed look.

Alex goes to touch his temple with an apologetic expression on his face, but he quickly lowers it when a cold splotch of clay touches his cheekbone. "Yeah, okay sorry, I should have announced myself." He's a little ungainly, but in an outgoing and friendly way—I've always liked him. I once overheard him explaining that he feels his personality is more appreciated in the States rather than back home in England.

"I was told to give you a message," he continues, rocking back on his heels, "in case you came in today."

"Oh yeah?" I try not to let him see me sweat.

"From Devlin." He leans in close and shields his mouth from the rest of the studio. "Or should I say *Devo*," he emphasizes with a knowing grin as I roll my eyes. "He wanted me to tell you that you should come to the studio tomorrow. He said he sent you a letter but wasn't sure it would get to you today." I narrow my eyes as I think that over. He's not here. Devo's not here but he wants to make sure I'm here tomorrow, and he used Alex as a back-up plan to make sure I knew that—that's thoughtful, I guess? So then why do I feel mad?

I try to keep all of that off my face while Alex assesses me. He cocks his head, knowing I've got a conversation brewing upstairs, but also likely knowing that I'm not going to share.

"That's it," he says, putting his hands on his hips.

"Well, thank you, Alex," I say. "You can tell him: 'message received'."

He shakes his head in response. "I can try but I barely know how to get in touch with the guy, I just email his assistant..." He looks to the side, then back to me with a grin. "I hope you two had fun yesterday." He waggles his finger at me, likely trying to get some kind of confirmatory reaction around the infamous Devo-Muse process.

Instead of responding to that particular instigation, curiosity strikes me. "What's his assistant's email?"

"Ehm"—Alex shifts from foot to foot—"I don't think I'm supposed to share."

"Alex," I say with a *come-on-now* look. "*Devo* and I are already in touch." Technically true, but through the US Postal Service. "I just want to send a thank you to his assistant, you know, for everything he did yesterday." Alex looks befuddled. I can read a stream of unasked questions in his eyes about what exactly transpired yesterday, but then I see him concede.

"Okay yes, that makes sense," he mumbles, wiping his hand on his smock repeatedly to get as much wet clay off it as possible before pulling his phone out of his back pocket. After a few taps of his thumb, Alex has pulled up the email. He looks up at me over his phone and mimics a stern impression. "But don't share with anyone else," he commands. I nod solemnly, then Alex reads out the email address.

That's the address I first used to contact Devo, I think. "Are you *sure* that's his assistant?"

Alex casts me some narrowed side-eye. "Yess," he drags out the single syllable with an arched brow, wondering why I'd question his direct answer. "I'm sure."

Huh. I think back to the request in our first snail mail exchange. "*Please don't respond to the email address moving forward.*" Then I think back to some of my discussion with Devo yesterday, when I'd teased him about his old-fashioned tendencies and Flintstones phone. He'd gone on about how our technology was changing the way humans interact with each other, "diluting" our artistic expression and chipping away at our attention spans. If that's really his assistant's email, then... *He really commits to being off the grid*, I think. I'm partially impressed that Devo practices what he preaches, but also partially horrified that my very first flirtatious message, intended for Devo, went to his assistant instead. I guess it got through the screening process.

I pinch the bridge of my nose for a moment to rid myself of that fresh embarrassment. Alex laughs awkwardly. "Uh, okay, C" —he bounces a step away—"I'm gonna go back to my piece before it cracks."

"Yeah, of course, go work on your piece!" I turn to walk away as well, a few steps behind him. "And thank you for the message."

"You got it," he shouts over his shoulder.

I breeze by my waiting canvas as I head out just to make sure there's no letter leaning against the easel. Nothing. I leave the studio a bit confused. A certain blonde's haughty gaze follows me as she looks out over her next flower painting. I do my best to ignore her, but I can feel her eyes boring holes into my back. *So much for 'fresh as a daisy,'* I think.

Chapter Five
THE REVEAL

It's Friday.

There's a small nest of butterflies in my stomach and as soon as I open my eyes and start thinking about the day, they make themselves known. I start rushing around my apartment getting ready. It's only 9:00 AM but I realize I was never told *when* I should be at the studio. I put my palm to my window, a lazy girl's guide to weather forecasting, and sense that it's chillier outside than the days prior.

I throw on my mid-rise army green jeans that accentuate my waist and a soft white button up that I *surreptitiously* leave unbuttoned around the top of my cleavage. I grab a silk kerchief with a gray and blue design on it and tie it cheerfully around my neck, leaving the tails dangling at the side across my collarbone. My hair is deciding to cooperate today, so I leave it undone, allowing my chestnut brown waves to fall across my shoulders and back. I go for full make-up this time, but still attempt an *I-barely-tried* approach. The main giveaway that I did, in fact, try was the dark pink lipstick swiped across my lips and my deeply lengthened eyelashes.

Ding! My heart jumps in response to the chime before I

remind my silly bodily reactions that Devo is not texting me. My number isn't programmed into the antique he calls a cellular device. When I unlock my phone, I see it's actually a mass text from Alex to the studio:

Hey everyone, it's Fri-YAY! I roll my eyes—what a goofball. The text continues: *Last minute announcement! (sorry, just got word!) At 11am today we'll be hosting a special unveiling of a painting from an artist I'm sure you've all heard of. A few members of the press will be in attendance, and they've been asked to feature a few of you and your art in their written pieces today, so come prepared! Don your nicest smocks and smiles! See you there! (There will be booze!) Cheers.*

I check the time and see we're closing in on 10:00 AM, might as well get a move on. I throw back on my pointed boots from yesterday, grab my navy peacoat, an overly ripe banana on its last legs, and then I head out. Because it's so chilly today, I opt to take the subway. I sit on the plastic orange seat, rapidly shaking my leg. I eat my banana like a monstrous toddler eating the head off a barbie doll. I'm sure as hell my demeanor isn't projecting ease. I make eye contact with a woman I presume is a tourist. She's eyeing my hunchbacked bouncing position and I look her straight in the eye during my next ferocious bite of banana before turning away like a feral animal.

What is going on with me? Sure, I'm nervous to find out how everything is going to unfold at the studio today. But I'm also more than a little peeved that I *don't know how everything is going to unfold at the studio today.* And maybe, I dunno, maybe I expected some sort of follow-up from Devo before the reveal? Some kind of backstage information, perhaps? Besides the sterile message from Alex, that is. Doesn't anybody get a girl flowers these days? I'm his muse for god's sake... *Aren't I?*

By the time I'm at the studio, a floppy and speckled banana peel hangs from my fingers and I'm all riled up. There are a few journalistic camps set up around the back wall of the space already, each with about two or three people, either conversing with notebooks in hand or setting up camera equipment on tripods. The room is even more full than it was yesterday—at least a third of the people milling about I don't recognize. So many more finished or half-finished projects are out on display, all facing the middle of the room, just in case an interested eye with a camera falls upon them. I squint, many people have taken the time to also place little makeshift name placards by their pieces. *Smart.* I eye my easel in the corner, facing the wrong way. *Eh,* I'll get to it later.

I waltz over to the kitchen to toss out my banana peel and find a cohort of artists, including Alex, Daisy and Miles mingling in a tight circle by the fridge. I'm not sure how much they know about Devo's painting and my involvement, but I suck up my instinct to avoid everyone and step into the gossip ring.

"He's Devo, isn't he?" I hear Daisy hiss.

"I can neither confirm nor deny the identity of today's special guest," says Alex, holding a mug to his lips and clearly enjoying being in the know.

"Come on, man! Tell us! It's our studio!" says a voice I don't recognize. I stand on my tiptoes to see within the small crowd better.

"Dude his paintings are hot." This time I recognize the voice—it's Miles elbowing the guy next to him. "I hear he fucks on the canvas," he says again. I roll my eyes but... he's not totally off base. I lower myself down from my tiptoes and put my head down. I realize I might not want people to see I'm listening in case they know anything about my involvement and want to ask questions. It's too late though, Daisy's eyeing me. She always notices me!

"He's been doing micro-residencies all up and down the coast," Daisy cuts in, switching her glare from me to Alex. She tosses shiny blonde curls over her shoulder. "Devlin... *Devo,*" she says with disdain. "Come on, it's like he's barely trying with his alter ego."

Rob walks into the kitchen at that moment, a bit more dressed down than the rest of us. He looks dumbfounded. "Ah, hey Charlotte." He looks around. "Heyyy everybody. Um, what's going on out there? I'm out of the loop."

"Dude, don't you read your texts?" Miles shouts.

"Ooo, no"—Rob sucks in air through his teeth—"I had a bit of a rendezvous this morning that took all of my, uh, attention." That probably meant he was just with someone from his long list of rotating lovers. He claims it relaxes him and puts him in the right headspace before starting his work at the studio.

Daisy cuts in, "We've been graced with the presence of a celebrity." Disdain drips from every word. I guess she still feels slighted by Devo's drifting attention at McArthur's earlier this week. She couldn't have known that we'd essentially been pen pals for weeks before he arrived. She never even stood a chance. I smile to myself, and I feel Daisy's glare again.

Alex finally takes control of the narrative: "We're hosting a press release for a special guest and holding space for journalistic coverage of the arts," he says with grandeur and checks his watch. "It starts in about five minutes, actually."

A quiet voice squeaks up from the crowd. It's a shy redheaded girl I'd seen around a few times in the last few months. "It's a Muse Painting, isn't it?" she says.

"Fuck yeah it is!" Miles gives the guy next to him a high five. Alex purses his lips and says nothing.

"What is a Muse paint—" Rob starts to mumble.

The redhead continues, "I heard each painting is based on a different woman. A real woman. Is it someone from our studio?"

I take that as my moment to turn on my heel and head towards the kitchen exit. I can hear Daisy's response behind me: "That's the rumor," she says bluntly.

As I stalk out, hoping no one puts together the timing of my exit, I look a few yards to my right and see a strapping figure in a form fitting, all-black outfit. He's wearing a baseball cap and is in a wide-legged stance, hands clasped low in front of him. A large object covered in a black fabric rolls up next to him thanks to a handsome young man with sandy blonde hair and a nose dappled in freckles. He walks back to the corner of the room in his khakis, and navy button-up. I stare for a moment too long and, as if he can sense my eyes on him, the sandy-haired man looks up to meet my gaze. He smiles and winks before focusing his attention back on the man in all black.

I think I just met Devo's assistant. I try to command my cheeks to hold in their creeping blush. A flash shakes me out of my head, and I realize there's a steady increase of clicks in the room as fancy cameras start to snap pictures. I don't want to be in these photographs, I realize. I head away from the kitchen to work my way into the crowd and have to skirt the figure in black to do so. As I pass, I take a deep breath through my nose. It's the smell of that woodsy aftershave and acrylic that gets me to turn around. It's him. Of course it is.

Devo stands there like a soldier next to a highly coveted object. Feet spread apart, hands held tightly together. His cap is pulled low over his face and his jagged black mask is pulled up and over his nose and mouth. He looks formidable, mysterious. I instinctually want to know what he's guarding. A slight upward tilt of Devo's head at this distance lets me see the slant of a stark blue iris. He sees me and the corner of his eye crinkles. Beneath that mask, Devo is smiling. He's smiling at me. I smile back and my blush is fully unleashed. In an effort to keep moving throughout this silent exchange, however, I forget to look where I'm going and nearly trip over an easel someone had hastily shoved toward the center of the room.

A man who I presume is a member of the press catches me by my forearm. "Woah," he says, "are you alright?"

"Yes, yes, thank you." I can hear Devo cough from a few yards behind me and I wonder if he's trying to cover up a laugh. *Bastard.*

Suddenly, Alex emerges from the kitchen. He claps a hand on

Devo's back who nods at him. Then Alex turns to address the guests. "Welcome everybody!" He has a booming voice when he wants to use it. I've always been impressed by that. No matter how awkward Alex can be at times, there's a reason he's become the de-facto representative of the studio—he cares, he buys in, he wants to keep the community together and thriving. He can command an audience, even if his speeches are littered with dad jokes.

"Thank you for attending our little gathering." He waves his arms around. "For those of you with your phones up, I'm going to ask you to abide by the honor system: Please don't upload any footage to social media, we've invited specific outlets here today for photographic coverage, thank you!" There was some murmuring in the crowd, but they all know that the limited coverage of Devo's paintings adds to the allure. The edges of the studio have filled out with those who were previously standing around in clumps. A few folks are elbowing each other and whispering, pointing to the object covered by the tarp next to Devo.

"As many of you know, we've been lucky enough to host a very, very special guest this past week." Alex puts his hand on Devo's shoulder again, who takes a moment to look up briefly at the crowd. Cameras snap, trying to get a glimpse of those piercing eyes. No wonder he prefers to keep his face in shadow —his heterochromia is striking in full light. Not helpful for someone who prefers to remain anonymous.

"Devo, is that you?" a member of some press contingent yells out.

Alex puts his hand out toward the man. "Don't worry, there will be time for questions in a few minutes"—he takes a deep breath—"but yes, you're stealin' my lines, man!" He gives a solitary chuckle. "Yes, everyone, this guy in front of all of you, looking like an international *super spy*, is Devo!" He smacks Devo's shoulder again, with maybe a little too much force. From my vantage point towards the front corner of the room, I swear

I can see Devo's eyes crinkle again as he subtly shakes his head back and forth.

So he thinks Alex is ridiculous too. We never had a chance to talk about that.

There's so much more we could have talked about. Like, oh I don't know, all our hopes and dreams and greatest fears, or whether he would forget me when he moves on to his next micro-residency. I take a deep breath. So many emotions are slithering through the block of nerves sitting in the bottom of my stomach: excitement, fear, jealousy, panic. I squeeze my hands together in front of me.

I've read all the articles that have covered his past micro-residency Muse painting reveals. I know the order of events—a brief introduction with a representative of the local studio and then a Q&A with the journalists representing various artistic publications, including popular blogs. There might even be a representative from *Devo's Darlings* here.

The door to the outside opens then, ushering in a sharp breeze that whips at my naked ankles. I turn. It's Marvin Flint. He works for *The New Yorker*. Geez. Being covered by *The New Yorker* Arts and Culture section is no small feat. I pinch the bridge of my nose and try to steady my breaths. All Muses have remained anonymous unless they revealed themselves, I remember. I won't be recognizable. Besides, I'm not famous, no one will care about my involvement. Except Daisy, I suppose.

"Now, before we reveal what we're all here to see," Alex retakes control of the murmuring crowd. "I'm going to give you a brief spiel about our humble little studio you're all standing in today. Copper Works, as its namesake suggests, used to be the final destination for details on fine copper goods! Nowadays, we host local artists working with all mediums, just for a small monthly fee. As an artist Co-Op..." I zone out, since I already know the history and set-up of our studio.

I can't stop staring at Devo—at his well-defined figure—just waiting there in that wide stance, head down. He seems so mysterious, and cold—nothing like the warm, charming and humorous young man I'd gotten to know in person over the past week. While his famous pseudonym and his real name are quite similar, this persona before me and the one who danced with me at McArthur's, who'd kissed the top of my head and held my hand, seem worlds apart.

I bite my lip.

"And with that, I'll hand it over to Devo and his team. He's been a delight to host and we're so excited to see his latest creation." Alex makes a grand sweeping gesture towards the shrouded object. Devo's assistant, waiting for his moment in the corner, walks up and very dramatically swooshes off the silken fabric. He quickly wraps the material around his forearms and retakes his silent post in the corner.

It feels as if my whole world narrows to the four foot by six foot canvas before me—before the entire room.

It's striking. The majority of the canvas has been hit with pastel blue splatters. It looks like hundreds of raindrops against a glass. Many of the drops have been set in relief by detail work I hadn't yet seen, with blues and grays of varying darker shades. It feels as if I'm looking at a three-dimensional background. Inches from the edges of the canvas, the green strikes begin—creating an almost glowing effect against the watery background.

Closer to the perimeter of the focal point of the painting are more pointed black splatters—they outline the curved figure of a woman on her side. Tangled tendrils of hair spill from the outline of her head towards the edge of one side of the canvas. Her head gives a tilted back impression, and the side profile of her face has been given more detail, including softly parted lips and eyes shut with light lashes cutting through the harsher black lines around her face.

One hand, fingers splayed, looks to be pushing its way through the canvas, right in front of the bend of her waist. Interesting, considering that I know my hands and wrists were dangling above the canvas, momentarily clasped in Devlin's hand.

Everything about the piece feels intimate and breathless. The background makes the subject feel wet and the tipped head and splayed fingers feel heady, desperate.

I suppose I had been.

I suppress a manic giggle. How wild that Devo's next muse, the Muse in front of us, is me. Just little 'ole me. It's beautiful, and there's no doubt that the painting is sensual and feminine... the subject had been admired. He'd done it again.

Cameras click and click. The room's initial murmurs have transformed into a cacophony of voices. Everyone is discussing the artistic choices of this piece compared to others in his series. A few folks are looking around, scrutinizing unknown faces, perhaps looking for the inspiration. But there are no identifying features on the woman captured in the canvas before us. It's just a figure in a moment of intimate pleasure. Forever anonymous unless she chooses not to be. That thought makes me feel powerful. I feel like I have a secret, and a memory I'll always cherish.

All mine.

And his.

I glance up to Devo. I wish I could better share this moment with him. His assistant is standing next to him, whispering. Devo gives a nod, then pushes the brim of his black hat down further.

Alex confers with them as well. "Alright, everyone, settle down!" He makes a gesture to imitate quelling the volume of the crowd by putting out his hands and lowering them. "It's time to take questions! Who's first?" He scans the room with a hand to his forehead as a mock visor. "You!" He points to the corner of the room farthest from me.

"Yes, Devo—is it true that all of your pieces are inspired by real women?" This question has been asked at previous reveals.

Devo's assistant confers with him for a moment, then speaks for him.

"Yes, Devo likes to draw direct inspiration from real life for authenticity," he projects, and then respectfully steps back, hands clasped behind his back.

The same voice shouts in response, "Well who's the lucky lady then!" My heart seizes. These crowds are normally a bit more polite. I try to mentally run through the written articles of these Q&As at previous studios. A name had never been given in connection with these paintings. But what if... no one had asked directly before? I squeeze my hands together tighter and note the short distance between me and the door. Only a few people to get around.

Devo's assistant goes to take a half step forward, but Devo gives a sharp shake of his head. Alex notices too. "Next question!" he booms. The assistant gives him an appreciative nod. "You!" Alex points to an older gentleman with a palm-sized notebook flipped open in the center of the room.

The man clears his throat and then begins, "This piece feels more intimate than some of your other pieces in this series, what was your relationship like with the subject?" The crowd goes relatively silent. Everyone wants the details on the Muse process. Me included. Based on the last question, however, I expect Devo to give a shake of his head—indicating a desire to move on to the next question.

I'm wrong.

He spends a few seconds conferring with the assistant, who nods solemnly. Then the assistant announces, "All of Devo's relationships with his subjects are..."—he hesitates, making me unsure how much artistic license he takes on these answers—"... special." I watch Devo's chest rise with a deep intake of breath. I don't know if that indicates frustration, resignation, anticipation... or something else.

If only I could see his face.

The assistant is watching Devo closely too. He finishes the

answer with a sharp eye on Devo's reactions, "But this was a particularly strong connection." Devo gives a diagonal tilt of his head—acknowledgement that this was true. I wonder how he would have explained it in his own words.

My heart squeezes again at this answer, then drops a few floors. If he feels like we had a "strong" connection... is it safe for me to admit to myself that I have a crush? Or will this man crush *me*. If all his Muse Paintings are created in a manner that's similar to this one... to *mine,* then this man's job is to be a literal playboy. I can't trust my heart with this. Best to keep my crush from leaving the stables.

A few more questions are thrown out from the audience about his methods and use of shadows in his splatter technique, which is apparently uncommon. A woman asks again about Devo's philosophy on depicting female pleasure. This is something he's answered many times, however, and his assistant barely needs to confer with him to give his readily recognized answer. "Female pleasure has been undervalued in our society and each person's pleasure is unique." I know all about this, so I continue to let my nervous thoughts run rampant through my head. Flashbacks to two days ago come and go. Me pushed against a doorframe, the silk tie sliding out from under my neck, his demand for me to remain quiet, *good girl.* My thighs squeeze together at the thought. I tune back in for the next question.

"You've completed twelve pieces in your Muse Series at local studios," a nasally voice says a few yards away from me. "Are you coming to a close soon? Will the series end? What's next?"

The assistant's head tips toward Devo and then he looks back up to answer, "This is all I'm at liberty to say: It will end. One day."

"*Great,*" the sharp voice mutters near me. Clearly not the answer he'd wanted. Nor the answer I want, I realize. My teeth clench as I bear the burning sensation washing over me. I'm just one of many, *with more to come.*

"You," Alex voices as he points at a newly raised hand.

"Will you ever see this woman again? This muse?" My breath catches. The seconds tick by at the same rate as my heartbeat. Time hangs suspended.

The assistant grins after conferring with Devo, and then he answers: "One day."

I'd been staring at a comforting scuff on the floor, but at hearing that response, my head whips up. The assistant's eyes find mine. He flashes me a polite smile and nods before quickly looking away. *What is* that *supposed to mean?*

The crowd starts murmuring again. Alex's booming voice goes a decibel above the rest, "And that's it for today folks! The Q&A portion has come to an end!"

The orderly ring of people around the room begins to loosen and the volume grows louder, but Alex isn't done: "For all our guests from the press, please take a moment to browse the room, we have many amazing local artists here today and much of their work is on display, please go ahead and ask them about it!" He adds the last bit in haste, "Anyone interested in ceramic sculpture, please see me!"

Alex never fails to take an opportunity, and I must admit I admire him for that. I look back toward Devo as he exits the room, assistant in tow. I don't know what to do. I want to run after him and look into his eyes. I want to pull down his mask and kiss him. Thank him for making my image so beautiful. But I also want to slap him—for not seeing me again. For *not* coming up to kiss me.

In my panic, I hesitate for too long and lose sight of him. Finally, my feet start moving and I'm cutting through the crowd. I walk past that same nasally voice I heard earlier, "...I can get the feature if I figure out who this guy is." My head whips toward the voice and I see a man sporting a mustache with twisted tips speaking to someone I presume is a colleague—a fancy camera dangles from his fingers. The two of them notice my stare and the mustache man looks back at me with narrowed eyes. Bad vibes. He gives me very bad, squirrely vibes.

I want to warn Devo.

I continue to push my way through the crowd, and I head in the direction I suspect Devo snuck down. I push past Alex, who's asking if I'm alright, and into the hallway that leads to the old loading dock behind the converted warehouse. I throw open the door to the cool breeze, but no one is there. It looks like the squirrely mustache man won't be getting the scoop he needs, and neither will I.

That night I go home and look up the meager footage of Devo's reveal today. Apparently just one rebellious, social media-savvy person had been there. The footage they'd posted had then been used over and over again on multiple platforms. One blogger had written up information on today's reveal, but no articles from any major arts and culture outlets or professional pictures had been published yet. It had only been a few hours. I refresh my email even though I'm pretty sure now the initial address I'd reached out to hadn't been a direct link to Devo.

Nothing.

I'd also checked my physical mailbox on the way in.

Nothing again.

I don't know what to think. I feel sad? No, I feel abandoned. Leaving today had been anticlimactic. Our studio group chat is blowing up. And I receive a text from Alex that reiterates what he'd asked me earlier today as I'd rushed down the hallway: "Hey, are you alright?"

No, I am decidedly not alright. I want to connect with the one person who knows what went into the reveal today. To the artist. To the mysterious, charming and frustrating man who had painted me *getting off* on a canvas.

Who gets to keep this mysterious image of me? Can only pop stars and art collectors afford it? I'll never see that painting in real life again. I wish I'd snapped a picture, but it didn't feel like something that would have the same effect through a screen.

I decide to lock the memory away. I'll take it out only when I feel like I can handle it. Or moments I want to reminisce... for simple physical reasons.

My throat feels tight and my chest aches. I can feel my body reaching out towards numbness to protect me.

My mind whirs into nothingness.

I close my eyes and go to sleep.

Chapter Six
THE AFTERMATH

I jolt out of bed the next morning at 7:55 AM to our buzzer going off incessantly. I hold down the ivory button that accesses the intercom and reply in a groggy voice, "Coming!"

I wrap myself in a robe, slide into my indoor slippers and go winding down the stairs. My heart is in my throat. I realize partway down that I'd jumped into action without thinking. What if I'm rushing down to some kind of early morning package delivery for Mariah? What if it's just some kid doing ding dong ditch? But I know what I'm hoping for... what if it's Devo? He did say he was an early riser... My palms begin to slide with sweat against the banister. *It has to be him.* The last few days had been so intense. There's no way he'd just disappear without seeing me in person, right? I hadn't even found the letter Alex told me Devo had sent days ago.

Partway across the second-floor landing, I find myself wishing I'd combed my hair and checked my appearance in the mirror. *Oh well,* I think. He can't expect a beauty queen at the crack of dawn. Once I get to the first floor, I can see a young man on the stoop with a messenger bag slung across his shoulder. He's bouncing up and down and looking around at the street, smacking a white envelope against his hand repeatedly. My eyes narrow, that's neither Devo nor his sandy-haired assistant. My heart drops for a moment, and then I eye the letter. That could still be from Devo.

"Please," I whisper before opening the door and holding my breath.

"Apartment 3D? Charlotte?" he inquires.

"Yes." I hold my breath.

"This letter requires a signature," he says, pulling out a digital signature board. I sign with one eye on the envelope, trying to see if there are any faint paint splatters across the back.

He hands me the envelope and then skips down the stoop, already headed to the corner. I examine the piece of correspondence and see that just my name and address are written on the front. No return address. No postage.

I head back up to our apartment and close the door, hoping Mariah went back to sleep after the buzzer alarm. Unable to wait, I sink down onto our kitchen floor and rip open the envelope flap with shaking fingers. Inside is a folded printer paper covered in black type.

Dear Miss Charlotte Faure,

It has come to the Zenith Foundation's attention that you have collaborated with the licentious street artist known as Devo. As our requirements indicate, the annual Zenith Award Recipient must comply with our standards of behavior within their professional body of work during their incumbency, which lasts until our next Recipient is chosen. Due to the public nature of the problematic piece of art, we must inform you that the Foundation is proceeding with an investigation around the revocation of your Zenith Award Winner status.

Sincerely,
The Zenith Foundation Committee

My blood is roaring in my ears. *Revocation??* What. The. Fuck. *Standards of behavior? It has come to their attention?*

I scan the impersonal typeface again to see if there's any language about a clawback on the prize money. I don't see anything... but still. Who are they to control my life? To take something from me that I had earned! And I collaborated with Devo anonymously! He'd made a point not to reveal any Muses. How could my participation in Devo's painting have been revealed? And to the Zenith Foundation?? I'm sure their members aren't avid Devo followers. They're all in their 60s and 70s—not exactly the demographic of his fanbase. They couldn't possibly know the *extent* to which I'd participated as a "muse"... could they? It's not like Devo or his assistant would have gone out of their way to sabotage the one artistic achievement I have on my resume besides school... *right?*

An image of narrowed hazel eyes and perfectly waved blonde hair swims to the forefront of my memory. "Daisy," I hiss. I couldn't be sure, but who else could it be—

"Morning sleepy head!" I nearly jump out of my skin as Mariah's cheery voice rouses me from my spiral. "Whatcha got there? Another letter from mystery man?"

Her words slice through me like a knife. "No," I bite back from the kitchen floor.

Mariah observes me for a minute, and I look back down at the paper in my hands, which I've now folded twice over. She tilts her head. "Is it something..." she hesitates, "that you want to talk about?"

I dip my chin towards my chest and avert my eyes while I try to avoid making Mariah a casualty of my emotions. "No. Thank you."

"Okayy. I'm here if you change your mind." She comes over and puts her palm on my head. I know she means it as a comforting gesture, but in the moment, it makes me feel like a dog. As if I'm someone's pet who belongs to anyone but myself.

I abruptly stand and Mariah steps back, still assessing me.

"I'm going to the studio today," I announce.

"Oh! You don't normally go in on weekends—"

"I know"—I cringe as I cut her off—"I just—" I take a deep inhale. "I need to get some emotions out." I gesture outward with my arms.

"I see that," Mariah responds. "Well, I support that decision! Art therapy is highly effective!" Her words float after me as I march into my bedroom to pull on more appropriate attire. I fling the Zenith Foundation letter on my bed and start getting ready.

Fuck this. Fuck all of this, I think.

"Oh! And I carried in another letter for you from our mailbox a few days ago!" Mariah says from the common space. "It's on the kitchen counter."

I hesitate, my leg partway through one side of my jeans. Then I continue my whirlwind of getting ready. "You can throw it away," I say on my way back through the kitchen to grab my set of keys.

"But what if it's sexy painter guy!"

I bite my tongue. "So what if it is," I say under my breath. I try to twist my features into some sort of half-smile when I turn back to Mariah. "See you later!"

I stomp out of the apartment in record time, having only done the basics. "Good luck!" I hear Mariah yell after me as the door closes. She doesn't deserve my snippiness, but I know she understands emotional reactions better than most thanks to her field of study. Once again, I recognize how lucky I am to have her as a friend, but sometimes I need my space. My fingers vibrate with the urge to pour my emotions out.

I text Alex on the way to Copper Works and he lets me know the location of the hide-a-key. "Glad to hear you're inspired to work!" he texts back. Ah, Alex, the ever-positive force in the world. I look around when I enter the studio and see that it is empty, nothing like the event from last night.

Instead, I'm reminded of the day I met Devo here. The day

we "collaborated." Against my wishes, my core heats up and my lower abdomen tingles at the memories. I grind my teeth as my body betrays me.

I eye the closet at the far end of the room and find myself walking toward it. Following a brief hesitation with my hand on the doorknob, I crack the door open and peek in. Then I open it wide. Still a normal storage closet. No couch, no carpet. No champagne. It's like I made it all up. I flick the door closed and suck on my teeth. *He's not here.*

I catch my reflection in one of the windows set into the concrete wall. My expression is blank. I move toward my canvas in the other corner of the room. Untouched for days. There's no note propped up on the easel.

He's not here, I think again.

I assess my painting and decide what I'd like to add to it today. In some respects, the painting could be finished. The central figure, the woman in the mist, is realistic—the details that make up her face are precise. Her features are pinched together as if they're in pain. I'd painted them using my brush with the finest bristles. The woman has one hand reaching toward the audience, completely clear of the swirling mist. With the other hand the woman clutches her charcoal gray jacket together at her collarbone. As I tilt my head, I wonder how much of this scene I'd pulled out of my head and how much I'd pulled out of *Pride & Prejudice*.

It's not what I want. There's emotion on her face, but the rest of the painting... it's emotionless. The craggy landscape she's in with the jutting greenery is painted *too* precisely. Even the mist, with it's white and gray swirls, is too perfect. I know I would have gotten an A from most of my oil painting professors if I'd submitted this piece, but suddenly, I hate it. *Devo had liked it,* whispers a little voice in my head. *Devo isn't here!* a more cynical side of me roars.

I go through the process of grabbing different oil paints and brushes as the irritable voice in my head continues. *He's not here and he's not coming back,* it hisses. *This is what he* does. *He goes from town to town, seducing women and selling their sexuality.* I know that isn't how I felt at the time, but the torrent of thought continues. *Everyone is going to find out about your promiscuity, your vulnerability.* My heart squeezes.

I sloppily tie my apron behind my back and roll up my sleeves. The flower paintings are still clothespinned to a wire in the corner diagonally across from me. *Fuck Daisy.* I dip a medium size brush in light gray paint. *Fuck Devo.* My hand shakes as I hover the brush tip before the canvas. *I shouldn't have gotten involved,* I think, turning my ire inward. *Shut up!* another part of me weighs in. *What's wrong with trying new things?*

Who am I trying to please? What do I want?

I press the brush onto the woman's hand that's reaching through the mist. It's the only part of her body that made it through the opaque wall of gray working to envelop her. It reminds me of the hand pushing through the canvas in yesterday's Muse Painting. Is this where he'd gotten the idea? So he stole some inspiration from me... why can't I steal some from him?

I smear the gray across the woman's hand and forearm. Now it appears that she's behind the mist, like she lives in it and she's peeking out at a world that's more clear, more defined. I begin mixing more shades of gray, blue and white. I use similar colors to what's already on the canvas to refresh the mist that takes up most of the background. When I'm done, I set my brush down.

I don't know what to do. I don't know what people want from me, or what I'm supposed to do, or how I'm supposed to feel.

I place the first two fingers of my right hand on one of the fresh swatches of paint in the background. I drag the wet paint over and up, spinning my wrist as much as I'm able to as I do, creating a swirl.

I step back.

It ruins the realism style of the painting, but that's what I want. I repeat the motion on another section of wet paint, this one more bluish—I hadn't mixed it into a perfectly natural color. I swirl the paint up and over the woman's head, nearly grazing it. Without wiping off my fingers, I do it again. To a whiter patch near the ground this time. And then I do it again. And again. A lot of swirls, some straighter smears. A couple of movements had even created angular shapes in the newly disordered sky.

I pick my brush back up and adjust the initial gray patch over the woman's previously outstretched arm.

I step back again. *One more thing.*

I take up my fine-bristled brush and go about changing the woman's expression. I don't want her to look distressed. I want her features to be smooth, and her eyes to be hard. She chooses to let the mist wrap around her—it's part of the landscape, and so is the nebulousness it brings. She can handle it. Whatever comes.

I stand back again and look at the new creation. The image is similar, but it's from a new perspective. The woman is in the mist, but she chooses to reside there. Nothing is clear or perfect, and the shapes that make up the mist continue to morph. But so can the woman, if she chooses.

It isn't what I expected to do. A part of me thought I might destroy the canvas and start again in order to make something even more perfect. But perfection is a subjective standard. This type of art isn't what's expected from me. It doesn't fit in with much of my body of work. It's not realistic. And while I'm used to painting tension, I'm not used to painting power. That's what's so uncomfortable about the woman's somewhat blank expression, I realize. Her world is in chaos, but she still has her choices. She knows who she is and she's not afraid.

The Zenith Foundation can have their righteous ideas of feminism and proper behavior, and Devo can fuck right off to the land behind his mask. I don't want to be confined anymore. I stand by my choices, and I will move forward in whichever manner I desire.

Chapter Seven
SEASONS CHANGE

Two Weeks Later

"Oh my god, Char! Is this you?" I can barely hear Mariah under my noise cancelling headphones. I peel one back and look over my shoulder. She's unfurled the almost six-foot tall canvas leaning against our kitchen counter.

I sigh and confirm, "Yeah, that's the one."

Last week, I'd finally sat down and filled Mariah in on everything that had happened with Devo and the painting. I gave her the high-level details, at least.

Right now, I'd very much like to get back to the sketchpad in front of me, but I know Mariah is going to continue.

"It's beautiful!" she exclaims as she goes to hold down the corners with cans of garbanzo beans and crushed tomatoes. I shrug. Although... even now, I can admit to myself that the painting is in fact, stunning. If you're into that kind of art, I mean. I don't know if I am anymore.

Devo's sandy-haired assistant had delivered the canvas late last Friday. I'd been wary of deliveries ever since my Muse Painting reveal. I wasn't in the mood to have anyone else weigh in on my lifestyle and choices via ominous letter.

From the top step of my stoop, I looked the assistant up and down with pursed lips. Devo, of course, was nowhere in sight. What could he and his *team* still want from me? My soul?

The young man and I assessed each other for a moment longer than what would be considered normal. He cocked his head as he took in my crossed arms and defensive stance.

"You must have made quite the impression," he started off.

I scoffed. "Says who?"

He went to scratch his temple and seemed to consider his next words carefully. "Do you, remember... who my boss is?"

"Yes!" I snapped. My poker face is often poor. I wear it all on my sleeve and everyone around me is in the danger zone until I stabilize. Guilt tugged at my heart—I knew he was just doing his job. "Yes," I managed to repeat more calmly. I smoothed my hands down my light-wash jeans "I do," I jumped back in before he could respond, "And I'm sorry, what's your name?"

"My name's John." He put his hand to his chest.

"Charlotte," I said, holding out my hand—my attempt at re-establishing some civility.

He took my hand but looked me in the eye as he chuckled. "Yes, I know."

My ears pricked with heat.

"I'm here because my boss wanted you to have this." He pushed forward a very tall cylindrical container with a white plastic cap. I grasped the cardboard tube from him in silence. "You can do whatever you want with it"—he waved at it—"it's worth a lot of money to the right buyers."

I had my suspicions about what was rolled up in the container.

"Why am I receiving this?" I said mechanically. Resistance stirred in my gut. I didn't want a *souvenir*. I'd wanted a conversation. Or even a phone call.

At this point, I wanted nothing to do with any of it.

"I don't know." John shrugged. "He normally sells his pieces and funnels the majority of the fee into the studio he held the residency at."

My eyes narrowed.

"He did ah, make a donation to your studio," he rushed to add, "but he wouldn't take any offers on the painting you two"—he scratched the back of his neck—"ah, worked on together."

How much did he know about how Devo conducts himself in these collaborations, I wondered. He seemed to know a lot.

I nodded, bordering on speechless.

"Thank you," I stuttered, not really meaning it and turning to head back inside.

"Wait!" John scrabbled to recapture my attention. "And he wanted you to have this."

I glanced back down at John as he held out a letter. *It's too late,* I thought. I took it anyway, nodded at John and headed back inside. I didn't look back to see what John's new impression of me was.

I hadn't cared.

It's been three days since that delivery and Mariah has just returned from a weekend away.

She'd been visiting her folks down in Virginia. Saturday was her parents' thirtieth wedding anniversary and they'd arranged for a nice dinner in their hometown. Mariah had sent me plenty of check-in texts while she'd been gone though, most of which I'd answered monosyllabically; at least I'd had the decorum to include *some* exclamation points.

Saturday, 9:05 PM:

> Hey Char! You doing things that bring you joy? <3

> Yup!

> Just remember, boys are bad except for dad!

> ...

> I mean, not your dad specifically. My b. It's just a stupid rhyme!

> Ok!

> Not everyone will abandon you!

> It's ok

> Ahhh! Sorry I've had a few cocktails with my parents. I'll be home Monday morning!

> Yay!

My weekend, on the other hand, had been one long hyperfixation on the new sketches that I might want to transfer to canvas. Without Mariah here to advocate for my mental health and forcing me to "spark joy," I'd barely left the apartment.

She's been back for all of two minutes and is already diving into things I've been avoiding for days. Mariah is currently kneeling on the ground beside the flattened canvas. I watch as she leans in towards different areas of the painting, taking in the detail—the splatters and whirls of blue, black, green and gray.

My heart squeezes at the memories of how I felt leading up to the creation of that painting. Lustful, nervous, safe, blissful... I'd mostly cycled through those, I think. It'd been a much more fun cycle than the last week or two—angry, numb, sad... determined.

At least this cycle had given me a kind of fuel. Before, I hadn't known how to get what I wanted, and I was afraid of losing something before I even had it. That fear had come to fruition. Now, I've fully let go.

"And you two no longer speak?" Mariah is tracing the implied tendrils of my hair with her fingertip. You'd think someone might be embarrassed seeing a depiction of their friend in the throes of sexual bliss. But that's not how Mariah works.

"Well, his assistant John did include this letter as well." I toss the sealed white envelope down from the counter and it lands beside her. I'd neither touched the rolled-up canvas nor his letter since I placed them inside our apartment on Friday. I'd been channeling my emotions into a new conceptual collection. Which is what I'd been working on in my sketchbook when Mariah had arrived.

I hear a gasp as I pick my way back over to my desk against the window in our common space. "You haven't opened it?!"

I shrug again, not really sure how to explain it. I think... I'm afraid of what it might say. Its existence makes my teeth grind and my heart palpitate. I don't want to deal with it.

"Well..." Mariah hesitates. "May I open it for you?"

"Sure," I release on an exhale. There's the sound of ripping paper and then, silence.

"What does it say?" I roll my eyes, already feeling myself rejecting the message.

"It says—" Mariah trails off for a moment. "It says, 'I'll come back one day. Hope you're well. XO, D'."

It takes a moment for the words to settle in my psyche. And then the teeth grinding intensifies.

Mariah flips over the paper and then looks once again inside the envelope. "Huh," she says, "that's it."

"Yeah," I deadpan, "that's it." I look at the painting, *that's it and that's all it ever was.*

Mariah takes in my closed-off expression. "It says he'll come back," she ventures. "That... is good! Right?"

"I don't care," I say. "I'm not falling for his mysterious vigilante persona anymore."

"Vigilante?" Mariah mutters.

"Whatever." I flick my hands in the air. "His whole charade! I'm out."

Mariah nods, letting me have my reaction. She decides to roll up the evidence of mine and Devo's "special" connection. "I'm just going to put this in the front hall closet then," she says softly.

"Thank you," I whisper. Once again, I don't deserve her.

I sit down at my desk in a huff. I'm on my fifth sketch of an image that had aggressively arrived in the front of my mind. It's a white marble statue of a woman from the bellybutton up. The statue is surrounded by red velvet ropes holding back crowds of people with cameras and cellphones held above their heads. A single tear runs down the sculpture's cheek and a hand with a chisel can be seen along the edge and away from the crowd, as if the sculptor had abandoned his piece. It feels modern. I'd never featured digital technology in my art before, but here we are. This is the world I live in. This isn't the Renaissance.

As I work on deciding whether there's a roof over the statue's head or just a chasm to the stars, my phone dings. I glance over and see I've gotten a notification from a dating app I'd downloaded out of spite. I'd been dissatisfied in more ways than one in the last couple of weeks. At least this part I can do something about.

I unlock my phone and glance between my sketchpad and my new suitor. His name is Anton. A tentative smile touches my lips as my eyes land on his profession. I'm in control of my new direction.

Let my next chapter begin.

Chapter Eight
EXHIBITION

Four Months Later

    I twist my hair up in what I hope is a fancy chignon. It feels like an artistic hair style, and if tonight's not enough proof that I'm a real artist, I don't know what is. On my way out the door I catch a glimpse of myself in the mirror. I instinctively smooth the natural ruching of my navy silk dress—I know it'll bunch up again as I continue to move around, but I can't help myself.

    My lips are a cool-toned dark cherry, and silver droplets hang from my ears. The earrings are literally shaped like oversized drops of water, and they glisten as I shake my head gently back and forth. A couple tendrils of my hair tumble forward out of my amateur chignon, but I don't try to tuck them back in. This is firstly because I don't know how, and I don't want to mess up the twisted hair that is intact. Secondly, the loose bits give me a slight girlish look, while the rest of my ensemble is more mature, woman-like. I think the juxtaposition suits me. I'm 27 years old, but I feel like I'm still coming of age.

    Maybe we always are.

    Alright you can reflect more later, I tell myself. *You can't be late to your own Exhibition.* I race downstairs as fast as I can in my two-and-a-half-inch heels, clutching the banister with one hand while my dainty black purse swings wildly from its silver chain in my other. Once on the sidewalk, I start to march in the direction of the subway, my normal route to the Lower East Side. But just as I get to the corner, a classic yellow cab comes toward me with its light on. If I want to romanticize my night, then this is too New York to ignore.

I bunch up the hem of my dress and hail the cab with my purse in the air. It stops immediately and I rush in. I haven't taken a cab like this in years. If I do wind up in a car, it's typically some kind of rideshare from an app. I let out a deep sigh and look out the window just as a few drops of rain hit the glass.

What kind of movie am I living in?? A smile creeps up the right side of my face.

"Where am I taking you, dear?" An elderly man with crinkles at the corners of his eyes and an impressive white beard turns around from the front seat. *Right*... I forgot that when you hail a cab the old-fashioned way, you actually have to tell the driver where you're going. My eyes widen as I try to remember the cross streets—that's what real cab drivers want to hear, right?

"Bowery and Stanton Street," I say. The driver turns forward with a hand hovering over his phone.

"Ah, just give me the address, that'll be easier to put into my map," he replies.

"Oh," I say, hand over my heart. I'm starting to get nervous about the evening. "The Rabbit Hole Gallery." I hope the name is good enough.

"Got it!" The driver taps on his phone and then we're off.

I look out the window again as more rain patters down the glass. I always thought that rain was rather romantic.

I can hear my phone buzzing in my tiny purse, but at this point, if something's gone wrong at the gallery, I'm sure Anton will inform me when I get there.

"So where are you off to all dressed up?" The bearded driver and I make eye contact in his rearview mirror. He seems friendly, and his aura puts me at ease. I can't say that's the case for every strange man you're trapped in close quarters with.

"I'm going to an art exhibition," I reply and smile, looking back out the window. "Paintings, actually."

"Ah, paintings! Beautiful!"

I give a small nod.

He continues, "Now don't you stray away from the pieces that make you uncomfortable! That's when your mind really expands." He makes an exploding motion with one of his hands off the side of his head.

"No, I won't," I respond. "I didn't." I say the second part just for myself.

We pull up to the gallery and I step out onto the damp sidewalk, careful to avoid the subway grate with my heels. "Thank you." I wave back to the cab driver as I go to step inside.

"Charlotte, Charlotte!" Rob comes bounding over. "You're never going to believe who's—"

"Ah, babe, there you are," says a silvery voice to my right. I look over and it's Anton, dressed in a deep maroon silk shirt, loosely unbuttoned at the neck, and a charcoal suit jacket. "I've been texting you." His voice is completely pleasant, but his smile is hard. Rob shies away from his presence immediately. Like a strong wind has blown his head back. I can see Rob's eyes flicking between me and the far corner of the room, but I feel like I need to give Anton my full attention in this moment. He's the gallery's almost-owner, after all.

"Is something wrong?" I say sweetly through my own smile.

"The number of pieces is wrong," he hisses. "There's a thirteenth painting hanging on the wall, and I don't know what to tell people about it. It doesn't fit the theme." He maintains his bright white smile and waves at an elderly gentleman as he walks in.

"Are you sure it's mine?" I didn't expect to be so stressed so immediately upon entering my own exhibition, but here I am. What if we're not even displaying my work? I look around and see the semi-abstract paintings I'd been working on for the last few months. Nothing looks out of place from this angle...

"Yes, your signature is in the corner." He points to a section of white wall freestanding in the middle of the room. "It's on the other side of that partition."

"Huh—" I start before I notice Anton scrutinizing me from head to toe.

"I thought I told you to wear the gold earrings I gave you for your birthday," he says, eyes narrowed.

"Mariah"—I grasp at an explanation—"she said these looked better." I touch one of the silver drops hanging delicately from my ear. That's a lie, but I don't want to argue with him right now.

Anton purses his lips before responding, "Well next time babe, listen to what I say, hmm?"

I nod demurely. Another elderly gentleman walks in. "I have to go say hi to my dad's contacts," Anton says, staring past me. He leans down to kiss my head without taking his eyes off the newcomers. "Big night, Charlotte!" he says as he takes off.

I release a breath I didn't realize I was holding and shake off the chill that had glazed my skin. All my friends should be here, Mariah should be here—she was coming straight from the university. My art is on the walls for the first time in almost two years. I take a moment to soak it all in before I click my way over to the area Anton had pointed to with the extra painting.

As I cross the room, I can see Rob watching me again from the far-left wall. His gaze is alternating between me and the location I'm walking toward. *Gosh*, I think, *what awful canvas of mine had they included?* Now Rob is leaning in close to Miles' ear and discreetly pointing. Miles is rubbing his chin and nodding, but then his eyes go wide, as if he's had a lightbulb moment. I'll have to get in on the discussion later after I figure out what to do about the incorrect piece.

Miles notices my eyes are on them and he awkwardly waves. Then his gaze flits to my left and I follow his stare.

A figure in a worn and oversized brown leather jacket has his arms crossed, leaning against the wall. One foot up. My first thought is to worry about a dusty boot print against the pristine white walls of Anton's father's gallery. He'll be very upset. But my next thought is that I recognize that stance—from the very first night I met... Devo.

I clutch the chain of my purse tighter and suck in my cheeks. Then, I meet his eyes. He has his head angled forward—his light brown hair is swept up off his forehead and his icy eyes are peering at me through long lashes. His lips hold the ghost of a smile.

How long has he been watching me? How long has he been here? Does he know this exhibition is.... mine?

He pushes off the wall and tilts his head to the side, walking toward me with a purposeful, unhurried stride. He's a little dressed down for this event, I realize, in his white T-shirt, beat-up jacket and Levi jeans. But still... there's something about the way he carries himself that makes me feel like a moth to a flame. Even if the flame is moving toward *me*, and I don't want to get burned again.

I school my features into a polite smile, pushing my genuine surprise to the forefront. Maybe I can hide my racing pulse with my raised eyebrows and a light laugh.

"Devlin!" I say in a sing-song voice. "So good to see you!" I close the gap between us and give him a hug like he's an old friend.

"Charlotte," he says in acknowledgement as he wraps one arm tightly around me, the other deep in his coat pocket. I step back and glance around, even though all I want to do is stare—bore holes into him with my eyeballs, in fact. *What is he* doing *here??*

"Good to see you too?" he says with a lilt on the end. This is not the way I'd expected to behave when I saw Devlin again. But then again, I planned on never seeing him again, so I hadn't thought this through. Now I find myself treating him like any other acquaintance you might run into in the aisles of the grocery store.

"Have you stumbled into the wrong gallery?" I ask innocently. There's no way he's here for me. His eyebrows knit together and his smile morphs into one of confusion.

"No," he says, assessing me as I smile sweetly. Like our moments of intense intimacy had never happened. Like he hadn't carried me in the throes of an orgasm onto a wet canvas. Like he had never had his face between my thighs or my wrists tied above my head. "I've finished the studio residencies I'd promised," he continues, "I came here for y—"

"There you are, babe!" The silky voice floats between us. It's Anton. He puts his arm around my shoulder, kissing my temple. There's a beat of silence and I realize Anton is staring at my new companion. He turns to me expectantly.

"Oh." I smooth down the front of my silk dress. "This is..."—I gesture toward Devlin, my mind racing—"an old colleague of mine."

"A colleague!" Anton's performance voice is three octaves higher than his normal speaking voice. He reaches forward for a handshake.

"Hey man, I'm Devlin"—he takes his hand—"and I'd say we were more like collaborators."

"Sure." I roll my eyes slightly as the blush I'd been fending off begins to show. "Collaborators," I mumble. Anton finally releases his hand and finishes sizing Devlin up, no doubt noting the lack of a designer label on his shoes.

Now it's Devlin who's looking at both of us expectantly. "Oh, and this is Anton!" I say, gesturing toward the man draped across my shoulders. I suck in my bottom lip as Anton places his outside hand across my collarbone.

"Luckiest man in the room," he says jovially. "I get to take home this lovely thing every night."

"Thing?" Devlin murmurs, his mouth twisting with slight distaste. I flinch, but Anton is already distracted, checking at who else is wandering in. I hadn't expected him to invite so many strangers. It feels like he's treating my exhibition like a networking event. I press my lips into a tight line.

While I did receive a chunk of funding for this collection from a few patrons, I suppose I don't know how I would have gotten into a gallery without Anton. That's why I was seeing him, right? *Right?* I was used for the sake of someone's art, so why can't I do the same for my art?

Before he steps away, Anton looks back at me suddenly. "Oh, Char!" I look up at him with doe eyes, not knowing what to expect. "Check out that piece behind us, huh?" He thumbs over his shoulder and we all turn to gaze up at the thirteenth painting he'd been fretting over when I arrived. "A mistake by the gallery technician"—Anton shakes his head as he offers this explanation to Devlin—"clearly doesn't fit the *theme.*" He draws out the "e" sound in annoyance.

The name of my exhibition is "Released," and nearly all my paintings clearly display that theme in their subject matter: there are figures who are walking off their canvas and depictions of flowing water and objects in flight, etcetera. The theme, however, isn't just embodied in the subject matter, but also in the methods I'd employed.

I'd always thought of myself as a realist painter. Figurative realism, objective realism. That's the style I'd always admired in my adolescence—the great Renaissance artists who painted such perfect human faces and perspective. But so much of the art I'd chosen for display is absurd and abstract. Like my *Woman in the Mist* painting, which is featured at the front of the gallery, many of the paintings have realism at their base, and then layers of abstraction. I'd felt like I'd unlocked new possibilities with this collection, like I no longer had to abide by anyone's standards. In many ways, I'd felt "released" from my assumed obligations.

My eyes widen though when they land on the additional piece. Anton's right, I hadn't intended for it to be included.

Devlin is looking at me with narrowed eyes and an open expression, waiting for me to speak on the painting.

This piece is not abstract, and I'd painted it in a private moment. It was two slender forearms pulled together at the top of the canvas and tied at the wrist. That was it. There was no face—just the feminine arms against a deep red background.

"Oh," I gasp and cover my lips with the tips of my fingers.

When I don't explain anything, Anton puts his head down to me and mock whispers, "A little private, don't you think?" He says it loud enough for Devlin to hear, who's observing everything very carefully. I even see Anton's eyes flick up to catch Devlin react, but Devlin's watching him right back. Anton nudges his shoulder and chuckles. "Sometimes we have a little too much fun, eh?" Right then, the one cater-waiter Anton had hired walks up with an aqua acrylic tray loaded with prosecco. Anton snags a glass.

"Well, it's very nice to meet you, David." He tips his head to Devlin and takes a gulp as he walks away.

"Gentlemen!" His voice carries back to us as he walks up to a circle of men with graying hair. I turn my head stiffly back to Devlin. I refuse to acknowledge his alter-ego, the one I'd had a silly girl's crush on all those months ago. Things are different now, I'm different. I lift my chin up once I meet his gaze, drawing in a breath.

Devlin glances between the painting and me. I hope he doesn't see it. Without a word, Devlin pulls something out of his pocket just enough for me to get a good look. It's a kerchief. My favorite kerchief, in fact. It was a creamy white with a pastel yellow floral pattern lining the perimeter. It's the same kerchief in the painting behind me. It's also the same kerchief I'd accidentally left with Devo after he'd used it to tie my wrists to the settee. That was something I'd never done before, and I'd liked it.

My chest tightens. I don't want to overreact in case I'm still being watched by the likes of Miles and Rob. To my knowledge, only the Zenith Foundation and the person who'd ratted me out ever found out about my participation in Devo's Brooklyn Muse Painting. But I'm sure there had been rumors in the studio, and I didn't need to feed them, even all these months later.

"You still have it?" I say, barely breaking my polite smile.

"You left it with me," he shrugs.

"You can have it," I respond before spinning to look back at the painting. Anywhere but his multi-colored irises. I'd found myself flicking between them, rememorizing their two shifting colors—one an arctic blue and the other a mint green. Both icy.

He steps up to stand beside me, looking at the painting as well. We both pretend it's supposed to be there, when in fact, it was supposed to be left behind. In the past.

"So, you and him"—Devlin tilts his head closer to mine—"this is something you do?" He gestures to the painting.

My limbs buzz with a righteous anger. "It's none of your business." I stay in front of the painting but turn my head to the side, looking away from him.

I can feel Devlin hesitate. Then he asks, "Does he know what he's doing?"

I snap my glare back to him. His audacity is beyond measure.

"Does he know what he's doing with *you*, I mean." He nods toward me.

I can feel my pupils melting into molten pits as I try to burn him down with my stare. My chest rises and falls twice before I've gathered myself enough to speak.

"Look, Devlin, what's in the past is in the past. You're not the only one who gained something from our..."—I wave my hands in the air and pluck out the word he'd used earlier—"collaboration." I jut my chin forward in defiance. "I learned what I want, and I pursued it. End of discussion. And his *name*," I finish, "is Anton."

A new wave of energy rolls off Devlin, but I watch him reign it in. He steers in a slightly new direction.

"So... Anton," he says, as if rolling the name around in his mouth. "He's your—"

"We're seeing each other," I cut in. I can see him nod out of the corner of my eye.

"Are you okay?"

Something about the tone of his voice, the lace of concern through it... it bothers me. I spin on my heel to face him directly.

"Yes, I'm okay." *Or I was, on my way here*, I think. "Why would you ask that? Why are you even here?" Finally, I break.

"I wanted to see you." The sincerity in his eyes is killing me. "I'd sent a few letters..." he lets out with a question in his voice.

Yes, I'd received a few letters with no return address, but whether they were from the Zenith Foundation continuing to tell me about my immoral, anti-feminist choices, or about Devo, the man who left me among the press and my floundering feelings, I hadn't wanted to know. Before Mariah saw them, I'd thrown them away. Instead, I'd googled his name and scanned the results just enough to see that he was seen at studios in different cities up north. Boston and then Portland, Maine. He was clearly busy, and so was I, I'd decided.

Thus, my release.

"When John told me you were having an exhibition, I knew I'd find you here." Despite my attitude, his eyes sparkle. "He's actually been asking after your influencer friend over there." He points to the far corner of the room, where John watches an overly enthusiastic Harper converse with two lithe and beautiful brunettes.

"I think he has a bit of a crush, actually," Devlin says, scratching the back of his head. "And so do I—"

"I don't know what you could possibly want from me," I cut him off with a hiss. This was a level of venom I didn't think I had anymore. But instead of stepping back, Devlin leans in.

"I'd *wanted*," he emphasizes, "to take you to dinner." I freeze. At this point, his head is so close to mine as he searches my eyes,

I worry that Anton will come back to claim what's his. I purse my lips and step back.

"I'm taken," I say stiffly. Then I jump to include, "I'm assuming you're not asking me as just a friend." *Why did I say that?* My cheeks must be cherries at this point. I was never good at holding my pride inside.

Devlin laughs in a way that unwinds the tight cords around my heart. It reminds me of when I'd met him at McArthur's and the carefree air he'd exuded then. It was intoxicating... and it still is.

"No, Charlotte. I wasn't planning on asking you as a friend."

I look between his amused eyes and shrug. "It's too late," I whisper.

His eyes harden at that. "My mistake," he says in a gruff tone. The amusement is gone. He jerks his chin at Anton's back, a few yards away. "Is it serious?"

Now it's my turn to be amused. "We, uh"—I fidget with one of my silver earrings—"only started seeing each other a few months ago. It's new—"

Devlin nods thoughtfully. "Do you respect him?"

My eyes widen at his new question. I open my mouth to speak, but nothing comes out. I stutter. Close my mouth and try again. There's a correct answer to this question, and I can't find myself able to share it. Instead, I just look at him with steely eyes, my shoulders tight and my lips drawn in a thin line.

He watches my every reaction, like I'm laid bare on the canvas again, but this time I don't feel as safe. He gives a solitary nod, as if I had, in fact, given him an answer.

"Beautiful earrings, by the way," he says, running a finger up to one of the silver drops. When he draws his hand away, he allows his forefinger to whisper along the curve of my jaw. A shiver wracks my body and I try not to let him see it. I fail.

"I'm going to be in town for a while," he says in a soft tone. "I'd love it if I could take you to coffee one day, as *friends*," he emphasizes.

I shake my head back and forth instinctually before I realize it. Then a "sure" bursts from my lips. Anton would never allow it. Devlin squints at the misdirection but then he smiles. His lips soft and full against his sun-kissed skin.

"I'm always up for a challenge, Charlotte!" He sweeps me into a friendly hug and then steps away. "Congratulations on your collection." He gestures around us. "Beauty is in the eye of the beholder, I know"—his eyes rove the space—"but it really is... undeniably lovely." He looks directly at me. For a moment, I'm entirely captured by his gaze. It feels as if he's trying to communicate through a look alone. Then the corner of his lip sneaks up and his gaze transforms from penetrative to conspiratorial. "This one's my favorite." He points at the wrists tied with the cream and yellow scarf. "And I think Anton's wrong. I think it does fit the theme."

My blush now extends to my ears, but I don't go to cover it, and I don't break our stare until I can't stand it anymore. I look down at the ground away from us, wondering how to escape this interaction. Before I can determine a parting line, Devlin does the honors.

"I can see I might have stirred up some unwelcome emotions." His hand moves toward my lowered chin, but then I see him think better of it and move it back toward his side. "And for that, I'm sorry. I will leave you to have your big night."

I nod in acquiescence, still looking down. *Finally, he's going to leave me alone.* I don't know how much longer I can hold any kind of mask in place.

"I'll send you a note, if you'll reply this time," he says softly. "I mean it about the coffee."

I snap my head up. "I can't always be waiting for you by the mailbox!" I say. "I don't have time for people who only communicate through archaic means." I wave my purse in the space between us.

Instead of laughing at my outburst, Devlin seems to consider my words seriously. "Noted," he says. "I'll have John be in touch, then."

I roll my eyes. So many barriers. Why does he think he's so special? I draw in a breath and bring my shoulders back, pulling myself together.

"Well, goodnight then," I say, chin up once again. He nods with a smile and then I turn away.

Mariah is three feet from me, staring. Her hand is at the base of her neck. Finally, a friendly face. I clip toward her, ignoring my desire to slouch which could be a gateway posture to curling up in a ball on the floor.

"Is that him?" she breathes. I nod.

"He seems to want you," she whispers looking over my shoulder toward the exit. I can see John push off the wall in my peripheral vision and I assume the two of them are really leaving. I sigh and then shrug at Mariah, shaking my head.

"I don't care what he wants." I stare at the wall behind her. "I don't *want* him."

Mariah eyes me skeptically. "Well, what did he say?"

"He said he wants to take me for coffee."

"Hmm," she acknowledges, a smile growing on her face. "So he's going to try."

I look up to the ceiling. "Yes, I think he might try."

Mariah giggles like a little girl.

"Now look who's the fangirl," I say, calling back to the days when she used to tease me for my foolish interest in Devo.

"Oh yes," she nods, her eyes still tracking the two young men walking out the door. "It's been fun to watch all the 'darlings' speculate."

I slant my eyes to hers with a raised brow, prompting further explanation.

"I take it you haven't been on *Devo's Darlings* lately?" she prods.

For the last few months, Mariah had been politely respecting my request to banish any Devo-related discussions between us.

Until now.

She takes in my pursed lips and otherwise blasé expression. Her eyes widen and she leans forward. I can tell she's deciding what to share.

"What?" I finally exclaim. "What is it? What are they speculating about?"

"Why he hasn't made any more Muse paintings!" Mariah finally lets out. I feel like her eyes are going to pop out of her head. She puts her hands on my shoulders and hisses, "The last one he made was of *you!*"

I blink, and slowly begin to uncross my arms. But then I think better of it and quickly wind them back in front of my chest, tilting my chin up.

"And then he came *here!*" Mariah continues. "To see *you*. It has to mean something."

I let the information settle for a moment.

"I'm taken," I say stiffly. *It doesn't mean anything then and it doesn't mean anything now.*

"Yes"—she puts her hand on my shoulder—"yes you are. And Anton... he's greattt." Her voice fades out, but then her eyes begin to sparkle. "But there's nothing wrong with a little competition."

TO BE CONTINUED...

Charlotte and Devo's second-chance love story is just getting started! Don't miss their next chapter in *Shape Me*, the second Muse Series book. Available now!

ACKNOWLEDGMENTS

I'd like to thank my wonderful cover designer Laura Rouw for her creativity, kindness, humor, and above all, for her patience! (What a weird job it is to be looking at Pinterest pictures of "forearm veins" together!)

Another thank you to my very first beta reader, Aimee, who —little known to her—was also the first person to ever read the manuscript of *Splatter Me* besides myself. Her feedback made me realize I could really do this (cue the tears of joy I cried in a hotel room in Dallas, Texas).

This next bit is going to be cheesy, but as I am writing these acknowledgements a few months after my initial digital publish of *Splatter Me*, I can now thank all the wonderful readers who have already taken a chance on this book, who reviewed it, DM'd me, posted about it on social media, recommended it to their friends, etc. I wish I could give each of you a big hug! You're the best!

Lastly, thank you to all of my incredibly supportive friends who have encouraged my writing, my creativity, and my head-in-the-clouds moments. I can't stop exploring made-up worlds, and I don't intend to :)

ABOUT THE AUTHOR

Missy Kaye is an author of fun-filled and high-tension romances that feature characters in creative scenarios. She aims to highlight characters going through their second "coming of age," because who figures it all out the first time?

Besides daydreaming, Missy also spends her time exploring New York City, collecting dating stories, and trying to convince her friends and family not to read her spicy scenes!

***

For more books and newsletter sign-up, go to:
MissyKayeBooks.com

You can also find me on instagram:
@missykayebooks

Made in the USA
Middletown, DE
26 July 2025

10583274R00085